CRACKS
IN MY
SIDEWALK

CRACKS
IN MY
SIDEWALK

JOHN C. WALL

iUniverse®

CRACKS IN MY SIDEWALK

iUniverse books may be ordered through booksellers or by contacting:

iUniverse
1663 Liberty Drive
Bloomington, IN 47403
www.iuniverse.com
1-800-Authors (1-800-288-4677)

ISBN: 978-1-5320-9328-9 (sc)
ISBN: 978-1-5320-9327-2 (e)

Print information available on the last page.

iUniverse rev. date: 01/21/2020

CONTENTS

FOREWORD

From time to time I enjoy looking back over my life's many memories. Historians say: You don't know where you're going if you don't know where you've been. Those memories inspired me to write this book.

When I was nine years old, my country was forced into World War Two. The surprise attack on Pearl Harbor gave us no choice. I wanted in that fight. I was mad, but I was too young. I had to settle for participating in scrap metal, tin foil, and paper drives as my contribution to the war effort. This was not very satisfying, but it had to do. Soon the men from my small town began to leave to join the fight. Some left as a group, such as the 45th division, part of the Oklahoma National Guard. Others left one, two, and three at a time as they became eligible. I knew most of these guys. I knew them well and admired their courage. Within a year, we began to receive telegram notices of those killed or missing in action. The town mourned with the families with each loss. When the war was finally over, men began coming home. Some had been highly decorated, and some had not left the country. Each person was given a hero's welcome; that was as it should be. Each was a hero, regardless of their duty assignment. They made their way back into civilian life with the same vigor and enthusiasm as they had when they left to go to war.

The book is a fictional story containing bits and pieces from my memory of the events during that era. It is written to honor the men and women who went and continue to go off to war and the families they leave behind. Throughout our history, they have sacrificed to keep our nation free.

Although this story is fictional, the theme could be repeated thousands of times through true stories in different settings. Many young men and women serving in the armed services have faced difficulties such as Robert Mitchel and met them just as he did. Perhaps you know someone from your hometown who fills the role.

CHAPTER 1

$\star \; \star \; \star$

The Landing

Time is drawing short. It's 6 June 1944. Bob Mitchel's landing craft has been circling, waiting for his turn to land on Omaha beach. Occasionally a shell explodes nearby, splashing water on the boat crew and troops. It's 0530, dusky dawn, and Bob could see in the distant view of the beach flashes of light coming from the muzzles of enemy guns. The sound from the battleship's sixteen- inch guns off to their right is deafening. It's apparent all hell is taking place.

Bob's mind strayed from the moment, "Can this be real? It seems only yesterday I was in high school enjoying a carefree life." He thought of his friends and loved ones. Mostly he thought of Jane, his childhood sweetheart he married just before shipping out and the letter he received announcing she was expecting their first child. "Will it be a boy? Two more months will tell. Will I be alive in two months? I wish I was back in Hugo, Oklahoma. The loudest noise you heard there was Howard yelling when his ace was trumped at the annual American Legion pinochle tournament." The shrill sound of a whistle brought Bob back to reality. It was time to align the boats and advance toward the beach. Bob's boat, along with eleven others, is in the second wave. The second wave is considered by some military specialists to be the most hazardous since enemy guns are sighted-in after the first wave has landed. By the time the fourth and fifth waves have landed, it's thought many guns will have been neutralized or silenced.

The coxswain turned the boat about and hollered over the sound of the engine,

"Have you got her set for battle speed, Bob?"

"You bet." Bob was in charge of the 225 hp diesel engine and the lowering and raising of the bow ramp.

As they approached the beach, small arms fire was whizzing over Bob's head; occasionally trails of machine gun fire could be seen ripping plumes of sand skyward. "Don't drop the ramp too soon," Bob kept repeating to himself. He thought if he could keep his mind on his job, he wouldn't be so scared. It was then Bob noticed the actions of the troops on board. "How can they be so calm while I'm about to pee in my pants? They've got guts!" He could hear some of the men praying softly. Others were sea sick and anxious to get on land, any land. Soon the boat was in contact with the sandy soil of France. As the ramp fell, machine gun fire brought two soldiers down before they could clear the landing craft. After completely clear the landing craft.

After the remaining troops had debarked, Bob picked up the two wounded soldiers from the ramp and placed them in the boat. He then dragged three additional wounded from the beach. The coxswain was fighting against the waves coming over the back of the boat, trying to keep it from broaching or turning sideways. That would present the enemy a big target; and most boats were hit while in that position.

"Bob, get back here and raise that ramp! Are you crazy? What's the matter with you? We've got to get out of here!" the coxswain screamed.

Bob raised the ramp just as the boat broke loose from the beach. He and the third crew member attended to the wounded men as they traveled back to the Bayfield, their mother ship. The wounded were off-loaded as additional troops descended the rope netting hung over the side of the ship. When they had a full load, they proceeded to the assigned area to circle and wait before returning to the beach.

"Here we go again! Still on battle speed, Bob?" the coxswain inquired.

"I'd have it faster than that, if I could. Let's get this over with," Bob replied.

Bob and his crew made three trips to the beach that day. Each time they brought back more wounded. Bob had gathered a total of nine men from the beach. On the third and last trip most of the small arms fire was directed away from the beach. The soldiers on shore were making headway and moving inland. Just an occasional burst of bullets could be seen hitting the beach. As nightfall came, all the troops and equipment aboard the Bayfield had been successfully transported. Bob's crew was relieved for some much-needed rest. It had been a long day. It was then Bob realized he had been hit in the arm. The bullet had not gone through his arm but grazed the outer skin tearing flesh away approximately two inches in length and one quarter inch deep. His shirt sleeve was soaked with blood. He had thought it came from the wounded he attended.

"Look at this. Talk about close. I don't even know when that happened," Bob said while showing his friends.

"You had better go to sick bay and get that looked at," they advised.

"Right now, I'm going to sleep. I'll wrap a clean "T" shirt around it and go in the morning."

The next morning Bob woke up with a throbbing arm. He skipped breakfast and made his way to sick bay. The doctor was not pleased that he had waited to report his injury. After cleaning and bandaging the wound, Bob was given some APC's and marked for duty. He asked the doctor about the wounded troops they had brought back from the beach.

"Was that your boat?" The Bayfield was designated as a field hospital ship for the invasion, but they hadn't expected wounded to arrive that quickly since the beach hadn't been secured. "The guys want to meet and thank you. Come on back, and I'll introduce you. Some of the more seriously wounded have been transferred to a better-equipped hospital ship, but I think they'll make it ok. One died on our operating table. Eight will live to see their folks back home. Good job!"

As Bob entered the recovery ward, the doctor announced who he was bringing by to visit. "Thank you! You saved my life!" was repeated by the two soldiers who had remained conscious.

"Guys, I'm glad ya'll are doing ok. You look better than the last time I saw you. Doc has fixed you up real good. Ya'll know there were two other guys that helped. If it's ok with Doc, they will come to see you later." Bob said in his cheeriest voice.

As Bob left, one of the patients said, "Doc, those guys should be written up for an award particularly the one who came onto the beach to get us. How he kept from getting hit we'll never know. There were bullets flying everywhere."

"They will be. I'll see to that. I'll need a statement from each of you. As a matter of fact, he did get hit. Not a serious wound. If I can keep it from getting infected, he'll be fine," Doc assured the men.

Several hours after the initial landing, conditions were such that wounded men could be safely transferred to the Bayfield for treatment. As corpsmen on the beach signaled for transport, boats were dispatched to pick up the injured. Although, the doctors onboard the Bayfield treated and saved many men; others were beyond help and died from their wounds. Their bodies were taken ashore to be placed in temporary burial sites on French soil.

Bob was among the boat crews tasked with ambulance service to and from the beach. Bob had been preoccupied about his performance under enemy fire; but now for the first time, he was aware of the devastation. "All those men killed! Torn to pieces! Seven of my shipmates killed and two missing! I had no idea what we were in for. Jimmy and I went through boot camp and Engineman School. To see him with half his body gone is more than I bargained for," were thoughts going through Bob's mind. That night Bob found a lonely area of the ship; he cried and prayed for those lost.

The Doctor and the ships Awards Officer interviewed all parties involved in Bob's rescue operation. They turned in a request for citations, but months would pass without word from the request. It was assumed after a period of time the request was denied, and the incident would be forgotten.

The Bayfield stayed on duty supporting the landing for several days. When field hospitals were established on land, the ship was relieved of hospital duty, and assigned the task of transporting additional equipment and personnel between England and France.

While cargo is being loaded in England, some crewmen are granted twelve- hour liberty passes. Bob and his close friends take full advantage of the hospitality offered at a service club near London which they had discovered even before the Normandy landing. Sandwiches, cake, tea, and coffee are available. A number of young ladies act as hostesses. It is made very clear that the girls are there to serve food, visit, and dance with the service men. If someone wanted a different type of female activity, they must look elsewhere. After Bob's friends have several sandwiches, they generally take off for more willing prospects. Bob is determined to be true to his wife and doesn't take part in their adventures.

"You guys be careful. There's a lot of trouble out there. I'll see ya'll back on the ship."

Bob enjoyed talking and dancing with the British girls. There was one girl in particular that Bob liked. She was an army nurse during the day and hostess at night for the USO. Gloria was her name; she was a well-educated woman, with a wonderful personality. Bob guessed that she might be two or three years older than he. They would sit for hours talking about home and their loved ones. Bob told her about his home town and how everyone looked out for each other. "If you and your husband are ever in the states, we'd love to have you visit. You would be our guests. I'd have your husband on horseback rounding up cattle in no time at all."

She laughed and said, "Albert and I would be honored, but I think horseback riding will take considerable persuasion. I'm not sure he would make a good cowhand." Gloria, like Bob, had only been married a short time before her husband left to join the Royal Air Force (RAF).

Sometimes, when Gloria is busy, Bob catches up on his letter writing. There are several areas in the club set up for that purpose. One night after Bob's friends had left, he began writing letters. After several letters were completed, he was tired and fell asleep. Gloria came to tell him they were closing.

"Wake-up, Bob, its closing time. Did you get all your letters written?" she asked.

"Oh! Yes, I dosed-off for a minute. Wow, I had no idea it was so late." he said looking at his watch. "Do you have a way home?"

"I don't live far from here, and I walk. It's nice out. If there are no bombs falling, I'll be ok," she answered.

"I'll walk you home. I don't think you should be out there alone. Too many slobs around, and I would never forgive myself if something bad happened to you. That is, if it's ok with you," Bob suggested.

"That would be nice. I'm ready. I'll get my coat, and we'll leave." Gloria answered.

On the way to Gloria's house, Bob didn't say much. He kept thinking, "What am I going to do if she asks me to come in? I could say it's too late. If I do go in, I wonder where it would lead. She seems to like me." Bob is a healthy nineteen-year old man who hadn't been with a woman in months. His male hormones kicked in as his mind considered the situation.

"Here we are. This is where I live."

It was a nice house with a vine covered entry and flower beds lining the walkway to the front door. They stood in silence for a moment. It was one of those awkward instances that people have when they want to do or say something, but are afraid to act.

"You didn't say much on the way here. What were you thinking?" Gloria broke the silence.

"I was just thinking about our situation and how much I enjoy being with you."

"That's nice you feel that way. I enjoy being with you too." Gloria answered

"Do you think a good night kiss would be ok?" Bob managed to get the words out.

"I would like that very much," she answered.

They embraced for what Bob had expected to be a short, impassionate kiss, but she melted in his arms. Their kiss was long as they held each other tightly. After their embrace they continued to hold each other, as if to extend, and savor the moment.

"It's been a long time since I was kissed, but never like that," she said.

"Me too," was all Bob could say.

"I know now what you were thinking on the way here. I could feel when our bodies were pressed together." She stated as she stepped back with a downward glance. "Don't be embarrassed. I'm aroused too!" She paused a moment, took a deep breath and collected her thoughts, "I'm not going to ask you in. Oh, yes, believe me I want to, but I know what would happen. I couldn't resist you. Tomorrow we would regret our night's pleasure." Gloria admitted.

"Gloria, I may thank you tomorrow, but right now I'm extremely disappointed. I've tried to be true, as you have, but I want you so bad." He waited for her reaction to his comment. When none came, he said, "If I was untrue, I'd want it to be with you. I think if we had met under different circumstances, we would have been right for each other." He paused again for her reaction. "Well, I'll get back to the ship now. We're still friends, aren't we?"

"You will always be more than a friend. I'm sorry to disappoint you, but it's for the best, good-night."

This would be the last time they would meet at the service club. Bob's ship sailed and did not return to England. They exchanged letters for several months. Gloria's husband was seriously injured and relieved from active duty. Her last letter was a request that he not write anymore. "I'm busy taking care of my husband, and I don't want him to get the wrong idea about our relationship. I will never forget you, and you'll always be close to my heart. Good-by dear friend, Gloria."

CHAPTER 2

✪ ✪ ✪

The Second Landing

The Bayfield was ordered to Naples to train troops for an assault on the southern coast of France. This time Bob made himself a promise not to become friends with any of the troops. "I'll be civil, but that's all. I don't want to look into the lifeless face of a new friend several hours after I've delivered him to his death." Many of the crew felt the same way and were struggling with the memory of the last landing.

With the training complete it was time for another invasion. The training paid off; all the troops and equipment were successfully landed. The fighting was not as intense as Normandy, but there were many casualties, including one boat crew. Once again, Bob's ship stayed on site for support until it was apparent the landing was secure.

The Bayfield had taken a beating and was scheduled to return to Norfolk, Virginia, Navy Yard, for repairs. When word of their destination leaked to the crew, they were anxious to write their loved ones. The wording in their letters had to be coded. Only a general idea of their movements could be conveyed. Otherwise, the censors would remove the sensitive words. Bob wrote, "You need to go see Uncle David for a visit soon. He will be happy to see you. I'm glad to hear he's been feeling better this past month." Many of the guys had given various areas of the world code names in order to inform loved ones back home what was happening. Bob's name for the east coast was David. Jane could tell that she was to go somewhere on the East coast in approximately one month. Air mail would be delivered much earlier than his ship's arrival.

The ship steamed into Norfolk on schedule and went in dry dock for sixty- five days. Each crew member would be given a ten-day leave, but was restricted to a one hundred mile radius from Norfolk. Bob called his wife and arranged to meet at a town sixty miles away. There were no rooms available in Norfolk. He requested his leave to start ten days after they arrived to allow travel time for his wife. Before Bob left for leave, his Division Officer instructed him to bring his wife with him when he returned. He was puzzled by the request.

"There are no rooms available here. I've tried." He responded.

"Don't worry about that. The Captain will take care of it. You just have her here on 15 September 1944 at 0900. Wear your dress blues and report to the O.D. on the Quarter Deck." was the reply.

"Don't worry! How can I keep from it? Am I getting arrested? Maybe the censors broke the code in my letter." Bob thought.

He was about to take off, but he couldn't stand the suspense any longer.

"I've got to see the Captain before I go on leave," he requested.

"Captain, I can't enjoy my leave unless you tell me why I'm to bring my wife back with me. Am I in trouble?"

"No, damn it. Son, I wasn't going to tell you. You're getting an award! I thought it would be nice if she could be here to see the ceremony."

"What a relief. Now, I can enjoy my leave. I don't know why I would be getting an award, but that's better than a court martial." He paused took a deep breath and said, "I was worried. With your permission, Sir, I'm leaving the ship. Thanks again, for telling me." Bob gave a snappy salute and departed.

The Captain laughed and said "On your way, sailor. Have a good time with your wife and that new baby boy."

Bob arrived at the bus station with a few minutes to spare. The station was crowded, but he worked his way to the refreshment counter. After a quick coke it was time to board the bus. There were times when

Bob wanted to kick the driver out of his seat and take over the operation. It seemed to go slower with every mile.

"Who put a thirty-five mile-an-hour speed limit on all vehicles? That's stupid! Guess it takes less gas." Like many service men that were stationed overseas, Bob was not aware of the rationing taking place back home. He was shocked when he learned that men stationed on shore duty in the states could sell coffee to make extra spending money. "Coffee is in short supply? We swim in it!" he thought.

"I hope Jane has arrived and located the place I arranged for us to stay. I know it won't be a nice place, but if it's clean and private, that will be good enough," were the thoughts going through his mind. He had obtained the address from a lady at the USO who helps arrange lodging for servicemen. "The lady said they hadn't received any negative feedback from the people she had sent there before. Surely the lodging will be ok."

"It's been over a year since we were together. From her letters she seems the same. I hope she will be as glad to see me as I am her. A lot can change in that time. What's the matter with you? Of course she will be." His train of thought was interrupted when the person seated next to him began to ask questions. He was an elderly man and seemed to be sincere in his admiration of the service men and women.

"I was in the last war. We pulled our artillery around with mules. Sure has changed. I tried to enlist, but they won't have me. I could have shuffled papers behind some desk, but "no!" I'm too old. Anyway, I thank you guys for doing the fighting. Kill one of them SOB's for me will ya, son?"

"Sure will," Bob answered. He thought this guy could talk them to death. However, it did make time go faster, and he was enjoying listening to the old man tell of his time in WW I. "I was stationed in France before......" the old man continued.

After a several minutes the man was talked out, and Bob fell asleep. Miles later, the driver nudged Bob's shoulder and said, "Fellow, we're here. There's a young lady jumping up and down waiting for you to get off this bus. Here's your luggage. Good luck, son."

Bob opened his eyes and was startled to see a strange man looking down at him. The stranger was dressed in a uniform Bob was not familiar with, and saying something he couldn't understand. It took him a few seconds to realize it was the bus driver. Until he looked out the bus window and saw Jane, he was in a daze. Fully awake now he rushed out the door. Everyone was watching to witness the reunion of two lovers. Some of the onlookers had big smiles on their faces while tears were running down their cheeks. It was a scene played over many times in the last three years. After a long embrace Bob's attention turned to his baby boy. A lady had been holding Joe while the two lovers kissed.

Jane introduced the strangers, "Bob, meet your son, Joe. I think he looks like you. And this lady is Mrs. Wallace, our landlord for the next few days."

"Oh! He's beautiful, Jane. He looks just like you. Hi, little fellow. I'm your dad!" Bob thanked Mrs. Wallace, and they left for their lodgings.

"You're going to love our place. Mrs. Wallace has an apartment over her garage. It has everything we hoped for. I have so much to tell you, and I want to hear everything you have done. I can't wait to get there. I'm so happy."

Bob was pleased with the arrangements; particularly the privacy. Mrs. Wallace offered to keep the baby if they needed time alone, but they were not ready to do that until they knew her better.

"Thanks, that's very thoughtful, but not yet. Bob wants to get acquainted with his son." Jane answered.

"When you are ready, let me know. I've raised three kids, and it would be nice to have a baby in the house again," Mrs. Wallace answered.

Joe was ready to take a nap, and that was perfect timing. Bob and Jane were anxious to start their second honeymoon. Actually, they didn't have much time together when they were married, only two weeks before Bob shipped out to the service. Joe slept most of the night. They didn't.

At 10:00 o'clock next morning Mrs. Wallace knocked on their door with coffee in hand. "I'll cook your breakfast when you're ready. Just come in the back door. It leads into the kitchen."

Bob and Jane were grateful. Although they had kitchen facilities, they had forgotten to get groceries. That would be high on their list of things to do later in the day. After a hot shower the three made their way downstairs. Mrs. Wallace was waiting at the kitchen table. "How do you like your eggs?" She asked.

While Bob and Jane ate, Mrs. Wallace told them she had two sons in the service. She had not heard from one of the boys in quite a while. He was overseas. Her other boy was stationed in Washington D. C. She said she treated her renters "like they're my sons. I only rent to service people. It makes me feel good."

"Is your husband working?" Jane asked.

"No, he passed away two years ago. He was sick for a long time. He fought hard, but it was too much. I do miss him so. But I try not to get down. My renters keep me going. I love meeting new people. Sometimes I get too involved in their lives. Actually, I've thought I should pay the renters for the therapy they provide."

"We're sorry to hear about your loss," Bob said.

They finished breakfast and went back to their apartment. They talked about Mrs. Wallace and how nice she treated them. They tried to think of some way to pay her back.

We'll let her keep Joe while we're here and take her with us to the park for an outing. What do you think, Bob?"

"Sounds good, but right now, why don't you get into that sexy night gown, and let's go to bed? I've always heard you can catch up in one day what you've waited years for. Well, I'm not caught up yet!"

"That sounds good too," Jane replied.

Later that day they made a trip to get groceries. Many things they attempted to purchase required a ration stamp or were not available. They reported to Mrs. Wallace about the problem. "I'll call the Ration Board and see if there aren't some temporary stamps they can issue. Surly they've had this problem before." She was instructed to have them come to the Ration Board office and bring a copy of Bob's leave orders. They received enough ration stamps for one pound of bacon, coffee, sugar and a one quarter pound of butter. With those items and the things that did not require stamps they would have enough.

Their leave was just about up. Mrs. Wallace asked where Bob was going after he got back. Before he could answer, she said, "Oh, never mind. I know you can't say. This war business has made it impossible to carry on the simplest conversation."

"Well, I don't know anyway, Mrs. Wallace. We don't get orders until we're out at sea. To tell you the truth, I haven't given it much thought," Bob replied.

Back in their apartment Bob and Jane were discussing that subject. "You know they wouldn't have sent us home for dry dock repairs unless we were headed to the Far East. There are dry docks in England we could have used. We'd better get a world map and do our code thing." They gave every island or group of islands a code name; from the west coast to mainland Japan.

"Panama will be the key. If I give you that code word, you'll know it's the Far East."

It was over. The time together they had waited for so long went in a hurry. They must pack their bags and prepare for the return trip to Norfolk. Jane was excited about getting to go back with Bob. It would be her first time to see a large ship. "If you think the Bayfield is big, wait until you see the carriers." Bob had checked the bus schedule and determined they should leave at 0500 the morning of the fifteenth. That would allow some extra time in case there was trouble on the road. They gave Mrs. Wallace the remainder of the sugar, coffee, and other grocery items they had purchased. They said good-by and thanked her for everything.

"Mrs. Wallace, could I write to you? I'll keep you posted on our family, and you can do the same. We want to know how you are getting along. If Bob is ever back this way, we would like to stay with you again," Jane stated.

"Of course, you are now one of my adopted families. Send me pictures of Joe, and I'll post them with the others on my Family Tree wall display.

It was a tearful parting. They had only known Mrs. Wallace a few days but had grown very close.

"She's like a second mother to me." Jane said, as they walked toward the bus station.

CHAPTER 3

✪ ✪ ✪

Homebound

The bus ride back to Norfolk was quick. Bob couldn't believe it was the same sixty miles. "Have they increased the speed limit? I thought the bus moved like a turtle on the way over." Bob commented.

Jane snuggled next to him, laughed, and said, "You were just anxious when you were on your way to see me." She gave him a kiss on the cheek.

They had breakfast at a small cafe outside the gate to the Navy Base. When it was near 0900, they left the cafe to return to the Bayfield. Bob and Jane climbed the gangplank leading to the Quarter Deck. He saluted the colors then the O. D, "Permission to come aboard, sir?" He reported in and was told to return to the car waiting on the dock.

"You're right on-time. The driver will know where to take you and Mrs. Mitchel."

"I don't understand all this. I've never been treated this way since I joined up. They've mixed me up with someone else. I hope you are not embarrassed before this is over." Bob told Jane as they approached Base Headquarters Building. A Navy Band from D.C. had just finished as they were getting out of the car. A Chief Petty Officer inquired who they were. He checked a list of names then escorted them to their assigned space in front of the stage that had been constructed for the occasion. Bob was seated on the front row while Jane was assigned a seat directly behind Bob on the second row. The second row contained people dressed in civilian clothes. Jane rightly assumed they were family or friends of those on the front row. Bob recognized many of his ship's company standing in formation behind and to the left of those seated. The coxswain and deck hand from his boat crew was seated several chairs to his right. There were five other sailors and one marine and two soldiers seated, but Bob did not know them.

The band continued to play several selections of music. "They're very good. I've heard the Hugo High band play some of those songs," Jane leaned forward and whispered.

At 0945, "Attention on deck" was sounded, and all hands stood immediately. Officers with gold braid, like Bob had never seen, came on the stage. After all had arrived, those with chairs were told to be seated, and the remainder to "stand at ease".

The Base Commander explained the purpose of the meeting was to recognize members of the armed service and present awards. "Presenting the awards is Admiral Norris, of the Eastern Naval District."

One by one each service man seated was called to the stage and given their awards. There were newspaper photographers, reporters, Life Magazine, and Time news-reel cameras recording each presentation. The two members of Bob's boat crew were given Bronze Star Medals. Bob was the last one to be called on stage.

"Attention to Orders! On 6 June 1944, 2nd Class Engineman, Robert T. Mitchel, serving aboard the USS Bayfield APA 33, rescued eight members of the United States landing forces at Normandy, France. During the rescue he was under intense enemy fire and placed himself in grave danger. He was wounded but continued to carry out his duties. He is awarded the Silver Star Medal for his heroic actions above and beyond the call of duty. In addition he will receive the Purple Heart Medal." The Admiral finished reading the orders and pinned the medals on Bob's chest.

"A final note: Lieutenant James Turk, who received the Purple Heart Medal earlier, was one of the men Petty Officer Mitchel rescued. He and his wife are anxious to meet you."

The attendees were dismissed and allowed to mingle. Several of Bob's shipmates came by to congratulate him. The rescued soldier and his wife occupied most of his and Jane's time. The reporters kept interrupting their conservation asking for their comments and pictures of Bob and Lt. Turk. The wives exchanged addresses and vowed to stay in touch by mail.

The Captain of the Bayfield gave Bob and his fellow crew members seven days liberty. Arrangements for pre-paid lodging had been made for Bob and Jane at the Roosevelt Hotel. The other crew members were single and left to their own discretion about lodging. However, all three had to report to the ship for one hour at 0800 each day so they wouldn't be charged leave time. Also, they were required to report by telephone each day at 1600 hour. At the hotel he was to inform the desk clerk where he was going and approximate return time.

When they were finally alone in their hotel room, Jane said, "I'm so proud of you, and I'm mad at the same time. You didn't tell me about that landing and getting shot. You better not do that anymore! I always knew I was married to a hero, but now everyone knows it. Did you know what was coming?"

"No, I was flabbergasted. When they first told me to bring you back, I thought I was in trouble. The Captain told me I was going to get an award, but I didn't know what it was for. I don't think I did anything all that great. It was a knee-jerk reaction. I saw those guys there. I knew I could get them, and I did. I don't think of myself as a hero. The one's still there are the heroes. Maybe the Navy went through this show to sell war bonds."

"Well, that soldier and his wife don't think it was for show. You're a hero to them and me too. Can you tell me what happened?" Jane replied.

"I will, but you must swear not to repeat what I say to anyone. Is that agreeable?'

"I won't tell a soul," Jane answered, with her hand over her heart.

Bob took a deep breath and began. "I think this may be good for me. I've never told my side of the story." He paused to gather his thoughts. "The first landing the machine gun fire was furious. Bullets were whistling over our heads when I lowered the ramp. The troops rushed to get off our craft. After all the troops had exited, it was my job to raise the ramp. When I started to raise it, I noticed that two soldiers had not cleared the ramp; their bodies were lying half on the ramp and half on the beach. I had no choice but to pull them inside the boat because I couldn't get a water-tight seal when I raised the ramp. There were two more bodies near the ramp. I pulled them in also. I looked toward the beach and saw a soldier sitting upright. He was about five yards away. He was crying. When he looked at me, I knew I could not leave him. I took both his hands and dragged him back. Bullets were flying all around us. I think that may have been when I was hit. After I got him in the boat, we discovered he had been wounded in both legs and could not walk. On the way back to the ship we applied tourniquets and pressure bandages that we made from cartridge belts and rope. We had to stop the bleeding. The second landing was much the same. I got three soldiers which were lying near the ramp. There was one other landing, but the shelling and small arms fire was almost non-existent. I got two more wounded while the troops were unloading the equipment. They had been attended to by a corpsman. He was probably going to come back and look at them later. I don't remember how many I pulled into our craft. I think it must have been around ten.

One thing that was never mentioned was Jim, the coxswain, was very upset with me for placing us in danger, particularly when I went five yards to get that guy. I think Jim would have left me if he could have got that ramp up. After all landings were completed, and we were back aboard the ship, he cooled off. I don't think he was mad. He was scared just like me. Well, that is the way things happened; now you, the Navy, and others think my actions were heroic; you point to those eight which were rescued. I'm pleased that they were able to go home, and I had a part in it." You look at eight soldiers, but I saw several others that I may have been able to reach, but they were several yards away, and I was afraid to try. That is why I cannot think of myself as a hero. I was scared all the time."

The next few days they enjoyed their extended time together. At Bob's request, the medal and the word hero were not mentioned again. During their stay they were treated with the utmost courtesy by the hotel staff and were served a free meal at the hotel restaurant. "This is embarrassing, but I must admit; it's nice. I haven't had a steak like this in months. Wait till I tell the guys. On second thought maybe I better not," Bob said with a sheepish grin.

CHAPTER 4

✪ ✪ ✪

Pacific Ocean

Bob's ship would leave dry dock in a few days and go out to sea. Jane would return to Hugo to wait for his next homecoming. She was anxious to show Bob's medals and tell everyone what had happened. Soon news reels showing Bob getting his medal were shown at movie theaters in Hugo. It also included a piece about the soldier Bob rescued from the beach. Pictures of Bob, Jane, Lt. Turk and his wife were shown shaking hands. The Erie Movie Theater offered free admission at special showings. Everyone in town attended.

The first letter Jane received after the Bayfield left Norfolk contained the code word for "Panama". She knew Bob was on his way to the Far East. The war in Japan hadn't been going well, and she was afraid for Bob's safety.

"Why couldn't he have stayed in Europe?" she thought. "We're mopping up there, and the end is in sight."

She wanted to talk to someone about his destination, but that was not possible. She remembered the War Poster "Loose lips sink ships." If she talked to someone, and his ship was torpedoed, the guilty feeling would be overwhelming. She would have to be content talking to Joe, since he was not old enough to repeat her comments.

21

The Bayfield joined a Task Group in San Francisco headed for Pearl Harbor. The crossing was rough. They were sailing in and out of storms typical of October weather in the Pacific. They had the equipment double lashed and life lines stretched along the upper decks. At the beginning of every voyage it was expected that a few of the ship's crew, and many troops would get sea sickness. This was true, in part, because of the first meal served at sea. The thinking behind that meal was: "It's going to happen, and we might as well get it over." Greasy pork chops and rough seas don't mix well.

Twice during their trip destroyers escorting the group indicated submarine contacts, and General Quarters was sounded. Bob's station was operating a diesel driven electric generator. It was located within the superstructure of the ship. Bob liked the location better than those stations located below deck. He waited anxiously for the "all clear" and was relieved when "Secure from General Quarters" was piped through the PA system. They learned later that one contact was an American sub and the other a false alarm. That was all right with the crew because they knew the destroyers were doing a good job protecting them.

After several days at sea the Task Group was near Pearl Harbor. Since there was a black out, they timed their arrival to enter the harbor during daylight hours. The troops were debarked and headed for Schofield Barracks. After all the equipment was offloaded, the crew was given a ten-hour liberty pass. The first thing Bob did was to mail his letter with the code word for Pearl Harbor. Bob and his friends walked about the base sightseeing. They had seen movies showing the destruction from the December 7, 1941, Japanese surprise attack. They were amazed at the progress being made cleaning up. Many of the ships which had been sunk had been raised and were being restored to service. The Arizona was still on its side. The sight of the once-proud man-of-war made Bob and his friends fighting mad. When they had completed the tour of the harbor, it was time to catch a bus going downtown for a few hours' relaxation.

There were a few bars and restaurants open for entertainment. They found a bar that wasn't too crowded and ordered drinks. They planned to have a few drinks and then find something to eat.

After an hour and a half, Bob said, "I'm going to that restaurant we spotted down the way and eat. I'm hungry!"

They left the bar in search of something to eat. Roger, who had drunk a bit more than the rest, wanted to find a girl named Mona Stover, that he heard about in the bar.

"Come on. You guys go with me. They say she is famous, and you can't be in Pearl Harbor without a visit to see Stover!" he pleaded.

"We're going to get something to eat. If you want to find her, you're going by yourself," they answered.

Bob and his friends were half-way through their meal when Roger appeared at their table. He was pale and obviously shaken-up.

"What happened to you? Did you find her?" someone asked.

"No! I had to go to the head in the bus station. I went to sleep, and when I woke, there were women chatting all over the place. A bus must have just arrived." Roger explained.

"You had gone in the women's rest room!? What did you do?" Bob asked

"I rolled up my pants legs and sat there. One woman kept shaking the door, saying, "Hurry up".

She must have looked under the partition and screamed, "There's a man in here!""

"Well, I waited for all of them to clear out. When there were no more sounds, I got out of there."

"That was close," his buddies chimed in.

"That's not all. There was a telephone booth just outside the restroom. I ran out and got in it. I picked up the phone just as two shore patrol officers came running by. They went in the women's rest room and came out after they found it empty. I could tell they were looking at me, but I just kept on talking into that phone. After a few seconds they shrugged their shoulders and left. I rolled my pants legs down and got out as quick as possible. Talk about sobering you up. Man, I'm sober. If ya'll don't mind waiting, I'd like to get something to eat." Roger finished.

"Go ahead and order. Did you really think you were going to fool someone with your pants legs rolled up? Those hairy legs, black socks and shoes must have given a clue that you were in the wrong place. Can't you guys imagine what that woman thought when she looked under that partition?" Bob inquired, smiling.

"I'm sure she didn't think it was Betty Gable." They all laughed at the mental picture they had of Roger's hairy legs exposed. They walked around town for a while and went back to the ship. It was a night to remember.

The work schedule doubled the next day, and everyone knew their stay in Pearl Harbor would be short. The crew was restricted to the base, but that was ok since they were too tired to go on liberty. The memories of their one night on the town had faded away except Roger's encounter in the ladies' restroom. Everyone on board had heard the story. Occasionally someone would make a comment about Roger's legs to get a laugh.

"Set the special sea detail" came over the PA system at 0800 January 16, 1945. They had loaded troops and equipment and were headed back to the war. Bob managed to write several letters during their time in Pearl. He knew once they left, it would be a long time before mail service would be available. After two days at sea they joined a task force made up of many different types of ships. The Captain announced their destination: "Attention all hands. We are headed for an island named Iwo Jima. It is a land mass vital to our plans for victory in the Far East. Upon arrival we will carry out an amphibious assault and land the troops of the 4th Marine Division on shore. The marines on board will take it and hold it. The Bayfield will remain in support of that landing until the island is secure. There will be additional announcements as we proceed to our target. That is all."

There is little leisure time aboard ship. The troops are having briefings on the upcoming landing at Iwo Jima. The ship's crew is standing watches four hours on and eight hours off. During the daylight hours, in addition to standing watch, boat crews are servicing the Gray Marine diesel engines. Everyone aboard has an assignment to carry out. Periodic announcements from the Captain keep everyone updated on the ship's location and the conditions at Iwo Jima. Upon arrival the Navy's warships have begun their bombardment of the island and will continue shelling until the landing begins.

"I'll be glad when we get there. I'm so tired, and hitting the beach will be a relief." Bob said.

"I think everyone feels that way. If being busy is supposed to keep us from thinking about what's ahead, it's not working. I don't feel good about this one. Are you scared?"

Roger answered, "Of course I'm scared, but I don't have a bad feeling. We'll do our jobs just like we've practiced. By the time we get there, you'll feel better," Bob encouraged.

The PA sounded, "All boat crews man your boats." The troops were told to gather their gear and prepare to move to their debark stations. The boat crews put their life jackets on and climbed aboard their boats. It was time!

"I have that rollover feeling in my gut that I had at Normandy. I don't know how to explain it," Bob said.

"You don't have to. I know what you mean. Me too. Let's get ol' boat Number 22 in the water. She has served us well," Bob's coxswain replied.

The crew hooked the crane to the boat and waited for the signal to be lifted over the side of the ship. Soon the speaker blasted: "Away all boats." The whine of the crane motors sounded throughout the ship. They were near the water, and Bob was ready to start the engine. A few turns of the starter, and the engine roared.

"I have sea suction, good oil pressure, battle speed setting, and we are ready to go." Bob reported to the coxswain. It was necessary to have sea water flowing through the engine to keep it from overheating.

The coxswain pulled away from the ship and got in line to pick up troops. With a full load of troops they headed for the beach.

The naval bombardment stopped as they approached the beach. Enemy artillery rounds were coming from a mountain at one end of the island. Little white puffs of smoke could be seen in the distance. It was obvious that the Japanese had been hiding deep within the mountain during the naval shelling. The naval bombardment resumed and concentrated on the mountain, away from the troop landing area. The beach was receiving less small arms fire, but more artillery shells exploding than they had in France. Shrapnel from a shell which exploded nearby entered boat No. 22 just above the waterline. The fragments went through the boat hitting Bob in the leg and upper chest. He wasn't in condition to lower or raise the ramp.

The coxswain told, Wendell, the deck hand, "Bob is hit; get back here and take over his duty."

The troops were off loaded, and they headed back to the Bayfield.

Bob was bleeding heavily from his leg. Wendell placed pressure on the wound to reduce the flow of blood. By the time they arrived at the ship, Bob was unconscious.

"Doc, he's hit in the shoulder and leg," the corpsman stated.

"Never mind the shoulder wound. If we don't get this bleeding in his leg stopped, it won't matter. Start a transfusion immediately!" the doctor said, as he worked feverishly to stop the bleeding. "Finally, well, that's done. How's he doing?" Doc inquired.

"His pressure is a little low but stable," the corpsman answered.

"Keep that transfusion hooked up. We may need more blood. Now, where are the x-rays of his chest?" The doctor looked at the x-rays. "We need to transfer him to one of the carriers flying patients out. His shoulder doesn't appear to have much damage, and there's little internal bleeding. That shrapnel needs to come out, but he's too weak right now. I'm not going to dig around for it. I'll contact the carrier, and you get him ready.

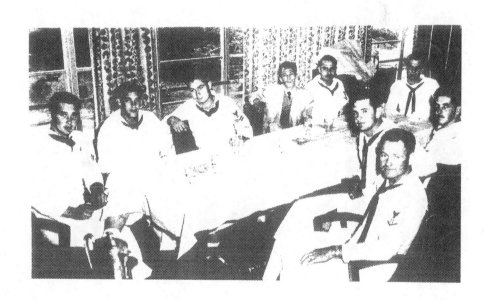

CHAPTER 5

❖ ❖ ❖

Wounded and Recovery

After a stop to refuel and change aircraft, Bob and the other wounded arrived at Hickam Air field in Pearl Harbor. They were immediately taken to the Naval Hospital. After several days rest the shrapnel was removed from his shoulder, and the internal damage repaired. Soon Bob was required to walk to the end of the hallway and back three times a day. This was very painful, but he was determined to get well. He knew that pain was part of the healing process. For the first few weeks he slept a great deal, but was getting stronger each day.

During his stay the Purple Heart Medal was awarded to Bob and his fellow patients who had been wounded in battle. This time there were no admirals to present his award. A few nurses, doctors, and photographers were in attendance. Bob seemed to prefer that. As patients became mobile, they would go throughout the ward giving encouragement to new arrivals. While making his rounds, Bob heard a familiar voice.

"Roger, is that you? Boy! It's good to see someone from the ship. Where did you get hit? When did you arrive? Where did the ship go when I left?" Bob was excited and full of questions.

"Hold on, one question at a time! Let's see, I got hit in the leg, I arrived yesterday, and I was hit during the landing on Okinawa. Ol' Doc aboard ship fixed me up as much as he could." He paused, "Bob, I might lose my leg. They're talking about it." Roger explained.

"Not your famous leg. Wait until I tell the doctor about your legs and how well known they are at the bus station downtown. He's not going to damage that image." Bob said cheerfully.

After they both laughed, Bob said, "Roger, I know this isn't a laughing matter, and I do take it seriously. Let's hope that it won't be necessary to amputate."

They had a long discussion about the ship, and what had happened after he left. Three members of "A" Division had been killed at Iwo Jima, and one during the Okinawa landing. "That makes a total of nine since we started out at Normandy," Bob said as he recalled each of his friends.

Every day when Roger would get back from the doctor's exam room, Bob would be at his bed. "What did he say? Is it looking better?"

"Yes! They won't have to take it off if it continues to improve," Roger said with a big smile.

"That's great! Since that has been decided, I'm going to tell about your encounter with the ladies' restroom. I think the guys will get a kick out of it. Besides, we have to get them rooting to save that leg too. I'm going to tell the doctors what they're dealing with. I know they'll do everything to save it, but it won't hurt if they know it's a famous leg they are working on. The pride of saving something known throughout the Navy may spur them on to do great things!" he added cheerfully.

"Haven't you told that enough? Crap, I'll have the most famous legs in the entire Navy before you guys get through. I bet they are repeating that story in my home state of Kansas. Oh well, tell it. I know you're going to, and you may be right. It may help." Roger reluctantly agreed.

Later, one of the patients drew a picture of a woman's rest room and added Roger's hairy legs, black socks and shoes with the pants rolled up. Everyone in the ward, nurses, and doctors signed it and gave it to Roger.

As time passed, both Bob and Roger grew stronger. "How would you two like to have four hours liberty?" their doctor asked.

"That would be great! When can we go?" they both responded.

"You can go this afternoon. I want you back by 1700. Bob, when you get back, I need to speak with you."

Bob wanted to go by the bus station and see the phone booth Roger had used to evade capture. He took a picture of Roger in the booth with his pants legs rolled up. "That will be one for the scrapbook!"

They spent the rest of their time outdoors drinking refreshments. They found a good patio table overlooking the beach. It was a good spot to observe surfers who were riding the ocean waves. There may have been a little girl- watching included in their entertainment. Bob and Roger had a wonderful afternoon on liberty. It was nice to see women wearing something other than a uniform. Bob reported to the doctor's office when they returned from liberty.

"Bob, you're going home. You will be transferred to the hospital in San Diego. Now, I'm not sure about this, but I think they will keep you for a very short time. They'll examine you, and if everything is ok, you will be discharged. Don't hold me to that; it's really up to the people there. Your chest/shoulder area has totally healed and shouldn't give you any trouble. Your leg will always be less than it was because of the damage to your muscles. It shouldn't give you any trouble, but you won't be as fast on your feet as you were. They might have you check in occasionally at a hospital near your home town, but again that is up to the people in San Diego. You've been a good patient and have been a big help with Roger. I think you had as much to do with saving his leg as anyone. I wish there was some way I could get word to your wife about your arrival, but there's nothing I can do."

"Don't worry about that, Doc. Thanks for everything. Take good care of Roger." Bob and Roger made plans to visit after Roger was discharged. "Just call the long-distance operator in Hugo, Oklahoma, and she will track me down. We'll set a time and place to meet then."

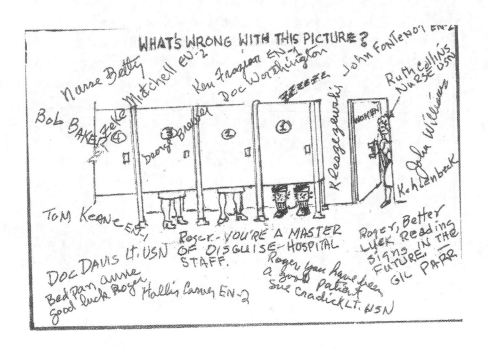

CHAPTER 6

✪ ✪ ✪

California Bound

I t was time for the coded letter. "I got three letters from you today. I'm glad to hear Joe is finally eating his vegetables. He must be growing like a weed. Your letter said he's gained weight every time you see the doctor. Do you still go every three weeks for his check up? I can't wait until I see him again. I know it's been hard raising him alone."

Bob knew Jane would not be waiting when the ship he was traveling on arrived in San Diego. Regardless, he spent several minutes looking up and down the dock for her. He was anxious to call home to see if she had received his coded letter.

Transportation was provided for Bob and several other patients to the hospital. The first thing he saw as they entered the hospital was a phone booth. The phone at his house only rang once before Jane answered. "Hello."

"That's a wonderful, wonderful sound." Bob said over Jane's scream.

"It's Bob," she announced to those present. "We have been taking turns sitting by the phone for three days. Where are you? How soon can I come to you?"

"I'm in San Diego. You can leave on the next bus. I'm stationed at the Naval Hospital in San Diego. Now, before you ask, I'm ok. They will probably only keep me a few days then... discharge!!!" Bob answered.

"Why are you in the hospital? Tell me now," Jane insisted.

"I was wounded in the chest and leg about two months ago, but I'm ok. I still have everything I started out with. Really, I'm ok," Bob knew she wouldn't be satisfied with anything but the truth. "Listen, there are guys waiting to use this phone, so I'll have to be quick. Catch a bus and plan to stay at least two weeks. I don't know when they will let me go. I love you, and I can't wait to see you. When you get here, ask anyone how to get to the Navy Hospital. Catch a taxi if you can find one."

"I was thrilled and shocked to see the word vegetables in your letter. And only three weeks away!! I already have the bags packed. I should be able to leave today or tomorrow at the latest. Shall I bring Joe or leave him with Mom?" Jane inquired.

"As much as I want to see him, you had better come alone. There are too many unknowns at this time. I don't even know if they would let Joe in the hospital, and we won't have a sitter here. It's just best. I'll call back and give your mother a phone number in case she needs to get in touch with us. Honey, I have to get off now. Tell all "hello" for me. I love you. Good-by," Bob said in closing.

"I love you too. And I'll see you soon. Good-bye."

CHAPTER 7

✪ ✪ ✪

Jane's Bus Ride

Jane left home the next day, and it was not long before she was reminded of Bob's comment about the bus moving like a turtle. She knew now what he felt. It seemed they stopped at every little town along Route 66. It would be a three-day trip, and she might as well settle in for the ride.

After two and a half days Jane was completely exhausted. She had had little sleep and only a few bites of food. When the bus stopped, there was only time for a restroom break or food. She always chose the restroom, but did manage to grab something to eat twice during the trip. It struck her odd that time on the road moved slowly, but like lighting during their rest stops. She was thankful that Joe was not with her. Bob was correct telling her to come alone. She arrived in San Diego around noontime and hailed a taxi. "I need to go to the Navy Hospital."

Jane stopped at the information desk and was given directions to Bob's ward. "Check with the nurse at the ward. She will see if it's ok to visit." The patients were eating and wouldn't be allowed visitors until 1400 hours. Bob had left a note with the nurse's station: "Jane, in case you get here at night, I reserved a room for you at the Howard Hotel across the street. The room is paid for, and all you have to do is check in at the desk."

"Since I have two hours; I'm going to check in at the Howard Hotel across the street. I've been three days on a bus, and I don't want Bob to see me looking like this. Can you tell him I'm here and will be back in a couple of hours?" Jane inquired.

After a shower and a fifteen-minute nap, Jane returned to Bob's ward, "Have you told him I'm here?"

"Yes, he's waiting in the visitors' lounge," the nurse answered with a big smile.

As soon as he saw her, he exclaimed, "I get discharged tomorrow, and we can start a new life. We're going to be the happiest couple in Hugo. I'm not going to have a serious thought for twenty years."

At 0900 the next morning Bob was a civilian. With his mustering out pay they had enough cash to look for a car. They found one that was in good shape and within their price range. Jane was pleased not to travel back on the bus. They packed the car and headed east. "Oklahoma, here we come!"

The trip back was wonderful. They enjoyed the cool air of the mountains, beautiful sunsets in the desert, and the view of grass meadows in cattle country near home. They soaked in every moment. It was as if they had never seen their country before. "Jane, there were times when I didn't know what this war was about, but I do now." Bob had pulled the car off the road and was looking at the blue sky, white clouds and sun deep on the western horizon. "Truthfully, I've always known, but this trip home is a refresher course for me. Our wonderful country and the freedom to travel it is what we're fighting for. Is it worth the cost? Oh, yes, and much more. Our freedom is not free. If they call me back tomorrow, I'll be proud to go! He paused, then with further thought, when I recall my friends and troops who gave their lives, I don't think I've done my share." Bob said as tears began streaming down his cheeks. "Jane, I'm sorry. I'm so ashamed and embarrassed, but I can't quit crying when I think about them. I should still be there.

Jane reached out to pull his head to her shoulder. "We've traveled far enough. Tomorrow will be a new day.

CHAPTER 8

* * *

Homecoming

There were approximately five hundred people waiting in Bob's parent's front yard when they arrived in Hugo. Among the greeters was the Mayor of Hugo, City Council members, Chief of Police, Coach Parker, County Sheriff, former school teachers and classmates. There were speeches, and refreshments in honor of a home town hero. Everyone had a wonderful time welcoming the couple home. Bob even managed to give a well worded "thank you" speech. After most of the crowd left, Coach Parker, Mayor Smith, and the Chief of Police all asked Bob what his plans were.

"I'm not sure. I think I would like to go to college over at Durant. I have the G.I. Bill, but that may not pay enough to support a family. I just don't know."

All three men told Bob, "Come see me when you make up your mind." They wanted to help in any way they could. After two weeks Bob and Jane had a plan, but needed help putting it into action. Bob asked Mayor Smith, Coach Parker, and the Chief of Police to meet with him and discuss his situation.

"I've been accepted to attend the university over at Durant. The GI Bill won't pay enough to get by. Jane and I will have to find jobs. We'd rather live in Hugo and commute because family and friends are here." He whispered, "Free babysitting" and laughed. I'd travel by bus three times a week the first semester, and be back in town around four. After the first semester I don't know what my class schedule would be, but it would probably be the same. Do you know of any jobs available here that I might qualify for? It would have to be part time."

All three men agreed that was a good plan. They were pleased he had decided to go to college. "We want you here in Hugo. Give us a few days. We'll get back with you. I'm sure we can come up with something suitable."

Bob thanked them and left. He told Jane the results of the meeting. "They said they might come up with something suitable. I hope they don't take too long. We've got lots to do and little time to do it."

Only two days had passed when Bob was summoned to the Mayor's office. The three men who had discussed his future were seated around a large table.

"Bob, have you had any experience in police work?" the mayor asked.

"I stood a lot of shore patrol duty in the service. That's the Navy's policeman. We took care of navy personnel if they got into trouble. We handled guys who were drunk and/or fighting mostly. Occasionally, we'd help civilians with directions or car trouble," Bob recalled.

"That's good!" Police Chief Baker said, "I've got a job for you. I need a man to help patrol the town on Thursday, Friday, and Saturday nights. You'd start at six o'clock evenings and quit around one in the morning. The pay is good. We can work that out later if you're interested. Generally, you'd be working with one of the deputies, but sometimes you may be by yourself."

"That sounds ideal. It would give me time to study and work into my schedule. The only problem I can see is making class on Fridays after being up until one the night before," Bob said excitedly.

"How about you work until ten o'clock on Thursdays? Would that be better?" the Chief suggested.

"Oh, yes. That would work fine. I'm very interested and ready to go to work any time you say."

"Well, that's done. Now, Coach Parker has something to offer." the Mayor said.

"I've spoken to Mr. Bowen. You may not know him, but he's the new high school principal. He's a nice guy. Anyway, he can use a part time helper in his office. The job consists of some filing, typing, and answering telephones, etc. If Jane is interested, she can call for an appointment to talk it over anytime during school hours."

"I don't know what to say." Tears were welling up in Bob's eyes. It was embarrassing, and he turned away while he composed himself. "I told the guys about Hugo and how everyone looked after each other. They didn't believe it. I wish they could be here now. Jane and I won't disappoint you. Thanks."

For the next few weeks Bob and Jane were in a tailspin. If it weren't instructions in law enforcement, it was classroom schedules. "I hope we get settled in our jobs before the semester starts," Bob said. "I have so much to learn. I didn't realize how much. It seems that it's mostly things not to do. I hope I don't get the city sued my first day on the job."

"You'll do fine. Just think of it as shore patrol duty," Jane replied.

"Well, I'm off for my last briefing, and then to work. This will be my first night alone. I'll call you about half way through the shift." Bob said as he left the house. The chief gave him his final instructions.

"Bob, as you know, there are several night spots in town. The Cottonwood Club is the most popular, but if there is trouble, it generally originates from the Bee Hive Inn. Remember their motto: "Bring Your Honey and Buzz Around." Sometimes their buzzing gets out of hand. That club will require the most of your attention. If trouble starts at any of the locations, don't let it leave there. You have all the information and training you need. If you get in trouble, call on the radio, and someone will be there immediately. Good luck, and I'm counting on you." Chief Baker gave Bob a pat on the back and sent him into the night.

Bob's first night was going smoothly. He had made the rounds, and everyone seemed to be having fun, and there was no sign of trouble. It was time to head back to the Bee Hive Inn. One of the bar girls called the police station, "I just heard three of our regulars talking. They plan to teach your new deputy a lesson. These guys are tough. You better get here quick! They have already have run all our customers off," she said and hung up the phone.

"Call the Chief. I'm on my way" the deputy told the dispatcher as he ran out of the station.

When Bob entered the club, the two brothers and their cousin approached him and said, "You think you're tough, don't you? We're here to show you you aren't as tough as you think."

"Well, which of you guys is going to brag tomorrow about three of you beating up one green policeman? That doesn't seem like much to brag about, but if that's what you want, let's go. Now, if you were to come at me one at a time, well that's different. There might be some brag in that." Bob said.

They thought it over and said, "Ok, Dunker, you take him first, but leave something for me."

By the time the deputy and Chief arrived; Dunker and his brother had re-gained clear heads. Bob had them sitting on the floor giving them a lecture. "Now, I didn't want to hurt ya'll tonight, so I took it easy on you. Had all three of you come at me at the same time, I may have hurt at least one of you very badly. I'm glad I didn't have to do that. Tomorrow when you're completely sober; think this over; figure out what you want. Heck, we might become good friends or at least we could learn to respect each other. Now, stay right where you are until I get back. Don't move! I'm going to talk to the owner and see if he wants to press charges." He returned shortly." The owner does not want to press chargers. Oh, almost forgot, since we had a confrontation, I must inquire if you need medical attention? After each responded "no". Bob said "good, now I was not trying to be a wise ass by asking that question. It is a requirement." I will be sore for a day or two as you probably will. After that time we should be fine." He paused, "I won't press charges. If you promise me you'll go straight home and stay there, I'll let you go."

"We promise. We don't want to spend the night in jail," they stated.

"Now this is a test for the future. If ya'll prove to be trustworthy, it might help you later. Do I have your word?" He waited to see if each one agreed. "Now we need to get a driver. I don't want ya'll having a wreck on the way home. You can come back in the morning and get your car. The bartender will have your keys." They all agreed, and thanked him.

The Chief and his deputy who had hurried to assist Bob stood in the shadow of the entry when they arrived. They could see Bob had everything under control and did not want him to know they came to rescue him. However, at this point they announced their presence and volunteered to drive two of the trouble-makers home. The Chief told Bob the next day he was very pleased with his handling of the situation.

The club owner made a special trip to see the chief, "Chief, I want your new deputy on my beat every day if possible. I never knew one man could do so many things with a night stick. I'm sure he could have hurt the guys by beating and hitting them, as I've seen in the past, but he didn't. He tripped, flipped, jabbed, choked, and made some other moves so fast I couldn't tell you what he did. The jabbing seemed to be his most effective action. On one guy he put his thumb under his chin and held one arm behind his back and had him on his tiptoes. He made him say, 'Uncle,' after which he set him on the floor. He put those guys' lights out so fast it was almost funny. They've always been a problem for me, but it will be interesting to see how they act now."

The Chief told the owner not to make fun or let any of his employee's make comments about what happened. "They were put down good, and it might be best if forgotten. We don't want to ruffle their pride any more than it already is. If you or anyone makes fun of them, that will be bad for my deputy and for your club. To answer your request, he will only be on duty Thursday, Friday, and Saturday evenings. He's going to college and has to study and get some rest."

As time passed, Bob's reputation as a peace-maker grew. Even the so-called thugs in town had respect for him. They weren't afraid, but they knew if they crossed him, they would have a big fight on their hands. All the law- abiding citizens and many of those he had arrested in the past would back him up.

Chief Baker wanted Bob to show all his deputies how to use a night stick "When I stood Shore Patrol (SP) duty in the Navy, I always dealt with the sailors as if our rolls would be reversed the next night. This could be true. All petty officers were assigned shore patrol duty. I always ask myself: How would I want to be treated? The answer to my question was: firm but fair. If you follow that principle, you'll be far ahead of the game. Remember we're not on duty one day and gone the next day. We're here for every day, and we must build trust and good relations." Bob illustrated different moves and tricks to subdue a suspect. "You must use a combination of kicks, fist, and night stick to be successful. Never rely on the night stick only. If you do, you'll get in trouble. I've seen some terrible injuries result from over-aggressive use of a night stick. I'm not saying you never hit to the head, but it would be a last resort." It was not long before those attending his lectures became very proficient handling trouble makers. As Bob's reputation grew, police and sheriff departments from near-by cities were requesting space for their personnel to attend his lectures. Bob was beginning to like law enforcement. Although it would add an additional semester before his graduation, he changed his class work to include several courses in law. "After all, we never know what doors will open or close in the future. I want to work at something I will enjoy and will make a difference in people's lives."

CHAPTER 9

✪ ✪ ✪

New Arrival

Things were going well for Bob and Jane. Their jobs were secure. Their financial situation was adequate. Bob's college work was doing well. His grades were exceptionally high. He thought he could have been a much better student in high school had he applied himself. "But, what the heck, you have to have some fun in life. It makes a difference though, when you have a family to support. I just needed to grow up." Bob hated to say that because he had promised himself not to have a serious thought for years after his discharge from service. Things were going so well they didn't have a worry in the world. This was about to change.

Doctor John's office was calling to report the results of Jane's physical. "Jane, are you seated?

She indicated, "Yes."

"Before I go any further," the doctor picked up his volume and said, "if our telephone operator is listening to this conservation and tells it, I will start some rumors she won't soon forget." About half way through his sentence, they heard a definite click. Doctor John and Jane had to chuckle. Doc indicated they sometimes attempt to listen to his conversations until he runs them off. "They hope to get an exclusive, but it's turned into a game. I can always tell if their mike is open. Rumors are easily started, but difficult to stop."

"Sounds like you put a stop to that rumor, Doctor," said Jane smiling.

He continued with the results of her test. "Jane, the rabbit died, or to put it another way, it would appear you are with child. I would estimate you're about two months along. I need you to come back, and let's double check before you make the announcements." There was dead silence. "Jane, are you there?"

"I'm here, Doctor. What a surprise!" she paused, "Should I tell Bob when he gets in?"

"Surprise! Jane, you do know what causes this," Doc said lightly. "No, I don't think I would tell anyone until we are absolutely sure."

"When do you want me to be back, Doctor?"

"Well, if you can wait until tomorrow, 9:00."

"I'll be there," Jane answered with a hint of a tear in her voice.

The following day tests were re-checked that confirmed Jane was expecting.

"Bob and I were intending to try for another baby soon. We wanted our kids no more than three years apart. This timing would certainly fit that criteria, but I'm not sure we're quite ready. I guess you're never fully prepared for this. I don't know how Bob will take this. Doctor John, you must think I'm silly."

"I think you are more in shock. I'll bet in three hours you'll be jumping up and down, and giggling like a school girl. When do you plan to tell Bob? She indicated they would talk that evening after supper. "I want to discuss this with both of you before this gets to be public knowledge.

"Why don't you come for supper tomorrow? We'll have fried chicken, biscuits, peas, salad, and whatever else I have left over in the refrigerator. How does that sound?" Jane replied.

"Wonderful. You know I can't resist a home-cooked meal. Since Mrs. John died, I don't get that home taste in food. I miss it, and I'll be there on time. I know Bob will need to study and I will leave shortly after our talk," Doctor John eagerly accepted.
"

After supper Doctor John said, "That was great Jane; you're a good cook. My wife Wanda and I couldn't have children, and we always said if we had, we would want them to be like you two. Except I would want you, Bob, to be better looking, look a little more handsome like me," Doc said with a laugh.

"I think Jane would agree with you on that good-looking business. Let's take our ice tea and go out on the back porch to talk. What did you want to say, Doctor? "

"I was wondering if you wanted me to deliver the baby. I realize you may prefer a younger doctor. If you do, I would understand."

"Of course, we want you to deliver our baby. You delivered Bob and me, and Joe is a fine healthy boy. Of course, we want you. You're our Doctor." Jane stated.

"You're number one in our books," Bob chimed in.

"That makes me happy, Jane; we will have to set up a schedule for your exams, and, Bob, I want you to come with her for the sixth month exam. By the way, have you thought of a name for the baby? Sometimes picking a name can be quite a chore. You know, I've always liked the name John for a boy and Jonett for a girl."

Bob and Jane looked at each other, grinned, and told Doctor John they liked those names too. "We had already decided on the name John David if we have a boy: John after you, and David after my uncle. We hadn't thought of a name for a girl, but we like the name Jonett.

"Once again, you've made me very happy. I'm going home and work out a schedule for "our baby." I'll call you tomorrow, Jane."

Jane hugged the doctor and said, "Now I know why your friends call you, "Doc number one."

"Very few know why they call me that, but it's not what you think. Would you like to hear the story? You'll have to swear not to tell." Doctor John said with a twinkle in his eye.

"We would love to hear the story!" Jane answered.

"Years ago, several of my friends were having coffee and conversation at Don's cafe when I arrived. The topic under discussion was T.W. Lambert. Each person told of his experience with T. W. and how he had managed to get the best of them during their various business dealings. When one completed his story, the others would laugh and indicate, "I can top that." They ranked each story by first, second, and third place based on who had been the most foolish and/or gullible. It was agreed that Gary Wallace was number one and was likely to stay in that position a long time. I listened intently and was amused by their tales of woe.

Gary asked me, "Have you had any dealings with T.W.?"

I told them that I knew T.W. when I saw him but had no contact other than a casual greeting. They warned me that if I should have any business dealings to be very careful.

"He will never get the best of me after hearing your problems. No, you can rest assured, I'll be extremely cautious," I replied with an air of confidence.

"Several months later T. W. entered my office early one morning. He told me that his wife was very sick and was wondering if I could make a house call. I asked what her symptoms were."

T. W. replied, "She's complaining about stomach cramps. She seems to be in real pain. What do you charge for a house call?"

"My charge will be $15.00," I answered. "This was $5.00 more than I normally charged, but considering whom I was dealing with, I wanted to be on the safe side. Also, I thought it would be only right for someone in town to get the better of this character."

"I'll pay you now. You will leave right away, won't you?" I assured him I would leave immediately.

"T.W. gave me $15.00 and said, 'I'll need a receipt marked *"paid in full"* for my records. If you put on there what it's for, that would be helpful'."

"I thought, that is a good idea. I want a full record when dealing with this person. I remembered the warning I had received."

"I handed T.W. the receipt, 'You can see it's marked, *'Paid in Full'* To attend to Mrs. Lambert—Symptoms stomach cramps'."

"On the way to Lambert's house I was very proud of the way I had handled T.W. I just realized that his initials probably stood for 'tight wad' and wondered if any of my friends had made that connection. I would ask later in the day. If not, I would surely receive their praises for having thought of it. I was certain they would be pleased about the extra $5.00 charge for a house call."

"When I arrived at the Lambert house, a neighbor lady met me at the door. 'Thank goodness you're here, Doctor. She's in terrible pain.' When

I entered the bedroom where Mrs. Lambert was located, I realized her "stomach cramps" were about to give birth. I spent the better part of the day delivering a six-pound boy. Several times I thought of the carefully worded receipt "Paid in Full. To attend Mrs. Lambert." I had spent all day delivering a baby for $15.00.

"The Lambert boy was about one year old before I could tell the story at Don's Café. From that time forward, my friends have addressed me as, 'Doc, number one.' So you see it sounds like a compliment, but it really isn't. However, I've had a lot of laughs. Don't get the idea that I dislike T.W. I think he is one of the best men we have in town. I'll tell you some stories about him and the good he has done for this town when we have more time. Now, I have to get home, and Bob you need to start studying."

CHAPTER 10

* * *

TW Lambert

It was time for Jane's six-month checkup. To this point everything had gone smoothly with her pregnancy with the exception of a few incidences of morning sickness. "I know we are a few minutes early, but we were anxious to see if everything is ok," Jane stated.

"That's fine. Hop on the scales, and we'll get started. Bob, I'm glad to see you could be here," said the nurse.

As the exam progressed, Dr. John said, "This is the fourth visit you've made to my office and haven't mentioned one time how you like the new clinic."

"It's a big improvement since Joe was born."

After the doctor assured them everything was fine, he said I told you someday I would tell you more stories about TW Lambert. If you have time, I think now would be a good opportunity to do that.

"Oh sure, we'd be glad to hear it!"

It was during the early thirties. Folks in Washington D.C. were calling it a depression. Those who worked for a living called it "tough times". Regardless of what you call it, several Hugo citizens were having great difficulties making ends meet. Mayor Jim Sanders thought it was time for action. He spoke to me about providing a helping hand to those in need.

"That's a great idea! We could ask Chief Baker and Coach Parker to meet and form a plan," I suggested.

"Why limit it to a few? It's everyone's duty to help a neighbor. Let's have a town meeting and enlist everyone. You know most will join and be glad to do so," Jim answered.

"You bet! There're good people in this town. Hold it!!! I see a problem with that idea. If we have a town meeting, T.W. will be there, and you know how outspoken he is. He's against everything. The old grouch! He'll ruin the whole idea. Before it's over, he will have everyone upset and have the town divided. Half the people will be ready to throw rocks at him, and the other half will be aiming at us!" I exclaimed.

"You let me worry about T. W. Get a meeting scheduled for next Tuesday night at seven o'clock. I'll act as moderator. Talk to Schooler about an article in the paper and get a few spots on the radio. I'm going to be out of town, but I'll be back for the meeting. Don't tell anyone, and I mean anyone, what the meeting is about."

The American Legion Hall was filling up. It was large enough to hold several hundred and a stage from which to address the crowd. Although Coach Parker, Chief Baker, and I didn't know the complete plan for the meeting, we had agreed to sit on the stage to show our support.

"Turnout is going to be good. I see T.W. has taken a seat on the front row. That figures," I said, surveying the audience.

"It's time to get started. Where the heck is Jim? I thought he was supposed to be the moderator," Chief Baker inquired.

"He was out of town day before yesterday, but he said he would be back in plenty of time to make this meeting. It was his idea in the first place. I can't believe he would be late. Let's take our place on stage. Hopefully he will show up by the time we get settled. If he doesn't show, I guess I'll say something first and call on you guys to comment on Jim's proposal. Ok?" I said reluctantly. I was thanking the people for coming and explaining about the moderator being detained when Jim appeared at the backstage door. His hair was uncombed, pants wrinkled, and shirt tail partially out.

"Well, folks, I spoke too soon. Here's your moderator right now. I'll turn the microphone over to someone you all know, Jim Sanders."

I whispered, "Thank goodness," under my breath as I was seated.

"Sorry I'm late, folks. I've had problems like you wouldn't believe."

T.W. hollered out, "We believe it. You look like the tail end of destruction. What have you been up to? No good I suspect."

"I know I don't look like much. Thanks for bringing that to everyone's attention." This comment drew a few laughs from the crowd as Jim tucked in his shirt and patted down his hair."

"Since you asked about my problem, T.W., I'll explain. Ya'll know I own timberland near Malvern, Arkansas. I was over there checking on the seedlings I had planted. I just got back late last night. My land is out in the boonies, and I can't find it without asking someone for directions. I stopped at a farm house where a man was standing on his front porch, and his little girl, maybe two or three years old, was playing in the front yard. He was getting ready to go to work in his garden and had leaned a hoe against the porch while he tied his shoes."

"As we were talking, I looked back in the direction of the road where he was pointing. When I turned to look, I noticed a snake several feet from where the little girl was playing. I told the farmer about the snake. It looked like a brown rattler commonly found in timberland. The man looked over my shoulder and said it would be ok. We continued to talk about the location of my property. Several times I looked back and noticed that the snake was moving closer to the baby. Each time I told that guy, he said it would be ok. I couldn't figure out why he didn't take the hoe and kill the snake. After all, the hoe was right there between us. By now the snake was only a few feet from her. It was so close I didn't want to look anymore and turned my back toward the child."

"I heard a scream. I jerked around to see what I already knew had happened. We did everything we could, but because of the location of the bite and her size, there was not much we could do. By the time we got to the hospital, it was too late. To lose a beautiful little baby like that was almost more than I have been able to take. Since then I can't sleep. I've tried to get it off my mind but haven't been able to. I don't know what's wrong with me!!" He paused.

"The silence in the room was broken by an angry shout from T.W. 'I know what's wrong with ya! You feel guilty, and by golly you should. You should've picked up that hoe and killed that snake yourself. I don't give a tinker's damn if that baby's father was there. That doesn't relieve you from responsibility. That baby was in trouble, and you should've helped'."

"Do you really feel that way T.W.?" Jim spoke in a surprised but apologetic tone.

"Yeah, I do!"

"Do the rest of you feel like T.W.?" Jim could tell from the lack of response and the fact that no one would look at him, the answer was, "yes".

"Well, I'm glad all of you feel like that. You're exactly right. I should feel guilty. When a person is in need, it is the responsibility of everyone to lend a helping hand. That is what this meeting is about tonight. Although, I made up that story about the little girl and the snake, we have the same situation right here in Hugo! There are people in need. It's time for all of us to do something about it. Turning your back on a problem won't make it go away. I want us to form committees tonight to oversee work parties, coordinate a food bank, employment agent, and any other committee we might see fit to organize."

"Now, we need to select a chairman and volunteers for the three committees I mentioned and, T.W., I would like for you to head up all committees. You would act as a chairman of the central committee. Coordinate their efforts and see to it that everything is working as it should. Will you do it?"

That night the ground work was laid for a very successful endeavor. All the committees were filled. Every person at the meeting volunteered to help. T.W. proved to be the right choice as leader for the program. He was a tough master-at -arms. If things were not moving fast enough, he would give a gentle nudge and say, "You've picked up the hoe. Now use it!"

For months he was never seen around town without a smile on his face, something the folks in Hugo had never witnessed before. "Helping people makes me feel good," he would say.

Since that time, TW has continued to help people in need, for this clinic was made possible by TW. The hospital your baby will be delivered in was due in large part to him. So you see why I think so highly of him in spite of my fifteen dollar delivery of his first born. The appointment ended with everyone laughing.

CHAPTER 11

* * *

Surprise Visit

Bob and Jane were pleased to learn the history behind the construction of the clinic and the hospital. They told Dr. John that their opinion of T.W. Lambert had certainly improved since they had heard that story. "I'm glad you feel that way; now let's get back to the do's and don'ts for the coming months." They scheduled Jane's next appointment, and everyone left the Doctor's office in a happy mood and looking forward to the arrival of their new baby.

The following day, Jane had completed her housework and sat down with a cup of tea when Bob came through the back door. "What are you doing, girl?" Bob asked.

"I'm taking a break, having a cup of tea and making some entries in my daily journal," Jane replied.

"Oh, I didn't know you kept a journal," Bob remarked.

"Yes," Jane replied, "I'm keeping track of all the good things and some of the not so good things that have happened to us through our marriage. I have quite a list on the good side, and a few on the bad side. In addition to my list, I also enter items of interest that happen during the day that seem important, thinking we may wish to recall these later on." They looked over her list and agreed there were certainly more good things that happened to them than there were bad things.

Bob said this reminded him of a story that his Grandpa had told him about the sidewalks in Hugo. He would stand at the end of the sidewalk and point down the way and say, "Son, life is like a sidewalk. It goes along real smooth, and then all of a sudden, cracks begin to appear because there's no good foundation under it. I associate those cracks with our problems in life. They are going to happen, but I'm going to tell you how to get through them. There are three things to remember: #1 you have to have a strong faith in God and, son, I think you have." Bob cleared his throat and continued with the story. "#2 You have to have a good education, and I don't mean just book learning. Study the people that you are around. See what makes them tick. Look at things from their point of view. Never stop learning. If you're ninety-nine years old, learn something new every day. And #3 Don't be lazy. If you take on a job, no matter what it is, give it the best you can. Son, if you do these 3 things, your sidewalk will be much smoother as you go through life."

"He was a smart man. I wish I had paid more attention to grandpa when he was alive." Bob laughed... "Come to think of it, I may have paid more attention to him than I thought, and that's why there are more good things than bad things in your daily journal. That's why our sidewalk has been so smooth. Let's get back to the business at hand."

"Now the reason I came by today, in addition to seeing you of course, was that I had two items that I wanted to tell you; however, I am uncertain which side of that list you would wish to put these," Bob stated. "First of all, the City Council has met and has voted to give me the position of Assistant Police Chief, with the thought in mind that when the existing Police Chief retires, which will be soon, they plan on moving me to that position. Of course this would mean more money immediately, but also more responsibility and more time away from home for me. I don't like the idea of being away from you more, particularly at this critical time. However, I assume you would put that on the good side of your list," stated Bob. "Now the other item is concerning a letter I received today at the office, addressed to: "Bob Mitchell, U.S. Navy Veteran, Hugo, Oklahoma". It was post marked from Albert and Gloria Simmons, General Hospital, Burn Center,

Houston, Texas. This is the lady I told you about that I spoke with frequently while I was stationed in England. Bob reminded her that he invited Gloria and her husband to visit them in Hugo anytime they were in this area. Gloria's husband, who was seriously injured and severely burned, had been sent to the Houston Burn Center.

"They are better equipped and have more expertise treating burns around the eyes and mouth than the British doctors," Bob stated. "It appears the Military is paying for Gloria's husband's care, room and board, and will also pay for her expenses once they have processed her paperwork. She was wondering if she could come here and spend a week or two with us while everything is finalized. Gloria stated she was running low on funds, and that she was not sure if this letter would even be received. She also said she certainly would understand if we were not able to host her during this time."

"Again," Bob assured her, "I'm uncertain which side of your list you would place this item on, so I am going to let you think this through and make a decision as to whether we should allow her to come up for a visit." Bob paused as he lovingly looked at his beautiful wife. "If we decide we should invite her, I would talk to my folks to see if she can stay at their place. They certainly have the room, and we don't, and I know they would be glad to have her. At any rate, take a few days and think on this, and we can write her a letter back with our decision," Bob suggested.

Jane responded immediately, "I don't need a few days; I can tell you right now I would love to meet her. I know she was a good friend of yours and meant a great deal to you. I would also love to meet her husband if he would be able to come up later! So, my decision is made right now; please write her a letter today and tell her that she is more than welcome to come here and see us, and I am tickled to death to meet her."

CHAPTER 12

✪ ✪ ✪

The Letter

After Several attempts, Bob had composed a letter he felt would be suitable to reply to Gloria's request to visit. Of course, he would have Jane and his parents review and give their approval. They agreed the letter was perfect after Jane had corrected a few misspelled words. Bob had purposely omitted the pending arrival of their second baby and that Gloria would be staying with Bob's parents. He did not want her to feel she would be imposing in any way. Bob had spoken to Dr. John regarding the stress of having company on Jane's health. When Dr. John was informed Gloria was a registered nurse in the English Army, he was pleased. "I think she will be a comfort to Jane," he said. "I don't know what the law is about reciprocity, but I will sure find out. Anyway, we will be glad to have her!" He laughed and said, "Don't tell her I'm going to put her to work!"

Bob felt like he had covered everything, and it was time to mail the letter. Bob instructed Gloria to call long distance collect and let them know when she would be arriving in Paris, Texas. This was twenty miles from Hugo, and the bus service between Paris and Hugo was not dependable. Jane and Bob would pick Gloria up and complete the trip. Bob thought it would take about four days to hear the arrival time. He went about his school work and police duties as usual. He would not allow this surprise visit to affect his routine, although during moments of quiet time, such as study, his mind wandered to his and Gloria's brief encounter. He had not recalled the incident for a long time, but now could remember every detail. Her soft sweet lips, the warmth of their bodies held tightly together, and their hearts pounding. He could remember it as if it were yesterday. It was a beautiful memory, but not one he wanted the opportunity to repeat. "I've got to stop thinking about this confound-it! I'm a happily married man!" After four extremely long days, word came that Gloria would meet them in Paris, Texas on Monday evening at seven o'clock. This was great because it was not Bob's night to work, and they would be able to get back to Hugo early in the evening. Everything was working fine until the unthinkable happened. Jane became sick and could not go! She said it was a little indigestion and suggested Bob continue and go by himself. Bob wanted to get a friend, or someone to go with him, but Jane insisted that would take too long. This was precisely what he did not want to happen. Somewhere rattling around in the back of Bob's mind was the thought that this was exactly what Jane wanted. Oh well, there was not time to give it much thought, but he certainly was going to ask her later. As Bob approached the bus station, he saw Gloria's bus had already arrived. By the time Bob had parked the car, Gloria had collected her luggage and was walking toward the station entrance. She had searched the crowd as the bus pulled into the station yet was unable to see a familiar face. She had seen pictures of Jane and was sure she would recognize either Jane or Bob. When she was unable to locate either of them, she became fearful. "What must I do?" She thought. In actuality, only fifteen minutes had passed since she exited the bus and gathered her luggage, but it seemed like a lifetime.

"Gloria," Bob called as he approached. She grabbed Bob and held him tightly. "I was so frightened. I thought I had misunderstood. I'm sorry, where is Jane? I must apologize!" Gloria was almost in tears. Her mind was racing—a strange country, little money, no one familiar, so many emotions welled up, and she was about to panic. No wonder she had grabbed Bob and held him so tightly.

Bob explained that Jane was ill and had not accompanied him. "I'm the one who should apologize for being late. You better not tell Jane;

she would get all over me, OK?" Bob said with a laugh. Then Bob said, "You haven't changed a bit. You are still beautiful. I would have known you anywhere!"

"Thank-you," stated Gloria. "I know I must look frightful after that bus ride. Is there somewhere we could stop for a cup of coffee and a restroom?" Gloria asked.

"I know just the place; they have good food and clean restrooms," Bob replied. They enjoyed reminiscing and bringing each other up-to-date on their activities. "I have thought of you many times and wondered how you and Albert were doing,"

"I have thought of you also. I know you and Jane are doing well from what you have told me so far. I'm so looking forward to meeting her," stated Gloria.

They finished their coffee and continued their journey to Hugo. They did not mention their encounter in London, but were certain the subject would arise at a later date.

They arrived at Bob's house around nine o'clock. Bob had explained that Gloria would be staying at his parents' house, but he wanted her to meet Jane first. Afterwards he would take her to his parents' house. Bob assured her she would be welcome there. When he turned into his driveway, he noticed his parents' car. "Looks like you will get to meet everyone at one time! My parents are here too," Bob stated.

As they entered, Gloria was greeted warmly. Jane and Gloria hugged. "I know we are going to be good friends. I can feel it already," Jane said excitedly.

"I feel it too," Gloria replied.

Bob's parents explained that they had been so anxious to meet Gloria. They asked Jane if they could wait for Gloria's arrival at her house because they knew Bob would come there first. Jane was pleased to have company. They laughed and talked until midnight discussing past and future events. They even spoke of the possibility of Albert visiting after his operation. Gloria was pleased and hoped it would be approved by his doctors. Eventually all were showing signs of fatigue.

"We better get this girl to bed, Bob," his mother said as she stood to leave. "We'll see you tomorrow."

CHAPTER 13

* * *

The British Are Coming

For the next few weeks, Bob, Jane, and Mr. and Mrs. Mitchel were busy introducing Gloria to the citizens of Hugo. Everyone Gloria met seemed to like her, and she received many invitations for lunch, dinner, and other activities occurring around town. One invitation she eagerly accepted was to speak to the world history class at Hugo High school. She thought it would be an opportunity to share information about her country. The students enjoyed her presentation and asked many questions afterward. They wondered about the after-effects of the war and the recovery process. Gloria was impressed with their knowledge of English history and current events. All the students loved her British accent. Some of the girls even attempted to imitate her speech, without much success. However, they did provide amusement and much entertainment for everyone for several days. No one actually laughed at them (except one or two boys). Most students and adults just smiled and turned away so as not to be seen.

When Gloria was introduced to the local physician Doctor John, she was surprised to find he had knowledge of her standing as a British Army nurse. He had made inquiries to determine the procedures required for her to serve as a nurse in Hugo. She would have to provide official documents showing her qualifications and her identification. Bob could be a witness if necessary. Her transcripts or some official documentation would be submitted to the County Health Department for approval. Doctor John told Gloria, "I feel sure it will be approved." The doctor continued, "If it is approved, I have a job for you, if you are interested."

"OH! Yes, I'm interested, you don't know what a relief it would be to know I will be able to work while my government gets the paperwork completed for my expenses. I have a copy of my license and military ID card. I'm so happy! I can't thank you enough," Gloria exclaimed! After she thought a few seconds, she stated, "You do know I may have to leave if my husband needs me."

Doctor John said, "I am aware of that and surely feel we can manage those times." They discussed her duties, hours, and salary. All the terms of employment were agreeable to them both. Doctor John said, "I think you will be ready to work in one or two weeks, maybe sooner." Jane was pleased Gloria would be her visiting nurse as they had already become good friends. Gloria might also assist Doctor John with Jane's delivery. Bob was also pleased that Gloria would be Jane's nurse.

"Jane, I'm the one who invited Gloria and Albert to visit. Practically everyone in town has taken her out to eat or to some activity except us! I know we have been busy, but I think it is time to be a better host," stated Bob. Bob then asked, "What do you think, Jane?" Jane agreed, and the arrangements were made to take her to Hugo's finest Italian restaurant, followed by a trip to Hugo Lake. Most everyone thought the lake was at its most beautiful at night with the moon and stars reflecting upon the water's surface.

Gloria informed them she had received a letter from Albert and needed to go to Houston in two days. Gloria stated, "I have arranged time off with Doctor John. Albert is between procedures and doing well. Don't tell anyone, but he may get to come back with me for a week or two if it is okay with you and your parents. I will telephone you if his Doctor approves his traveling," Gloria stated with a tone of joy.

Bob and Jane were thrilled at the prospect of meeting Albert at last. Gloria left for Houston, and once again the Mitchel family waited anxiously for a telephone call.

When the call finally came, Jane answered, "Hello?", it was Gloria's voice speaking excitedly. "He is coming with me! Albert is going to come and stay a little over a week, or two or three if it's ok!" She related some of the conditions; "he would have to see Doctor John every other day. The doctors at Houston have spoken to Doctor John, and they have reached an agreement. Isn't this Wonderful? He wants to ride a horse and rope a cow if that can be arranged," Gloria stated.

Jane laughed. They discussed arrival times and all the necessary details and ended their conversation on a happy note. Upon his arrival, Albert was received by the citizens of Hugo with open arms, just as his lovely wife had been. He was asked to speak at a meeting at the American Legion Hall. His speech was a success, and afterwards the emcee told the crowd about Albert's wish to ride a horse and rope a cow. The American Legion members presented him with a Stetson hat and boots for the occasion. Other town merchants ensured he had blue jeans and a western shirt. Albert thanked them many times and placed the Stetson hat on his head, much to the pleasure of the audience. Bob borrowed a gentle roping horse, which Albert practiced riding while twirling a lariat over the horse's head. After two days, he declared himself ready. Bob put a young calf in a small enclosure measuring about 25 yards by 50 yards. Albert chased that calf all over that pen. He threw the lariat several times. The first time he almost roped his own horse! Each time he tried, the large crowd gave him encouragement. He was not going to give up. After the calf was completely exhausted and providing a practically still target, Albert attempted his sixth try, which roped the calf perfectly. The roar from the crowd was deafening! Bob had a photographer standing by to document this great occasion. The picture was featured on the front page of the Hugo Daily News the next day. Everyone was so proud of Albert, Gloria most of all! Albert and Gloria's time in Hugo had come to an end. Gloria sorrowfully told Jane, "I don't think I will be coming back; I'm certain they will release him and send us home." Gloria continued, "One of the things I regret most is not being able to stay and assist Doctor John with the delivery of your precious baby." (Which Jane delivered two weeks later, a 6 pound, 8 ounce healthy baby boy). Most everyone in town was there for Albert and Gloria's going-away party. Even the Hugo High School Band was there to join in the send-off. Many tears flowed that day, and it took Hugo a long time to return to normal after their departure.

Bob and Jane stayed in touch with Albert and Gloria the rest of their lives mostly via mail, even once meeting at a Veteran's reunion in France.

CHAPTER 14

* * *

Chief Justice

Bob was suddenly promoted to chief of police due to the illness of Chief Baker. His promotion surprised no one since the city council had already nominated him for that position. Advancing had not been difficult for Bob. He was aware of and had performed most of his required duties with the exception of managing the financial and personnel needs of the department. In addition to his knowledge of the work, his greatest asset was his personality. He was well-liked by the town's people and respected by the law enforcement community. When he introduced changes or added some of his new methods of operation, he was rarely questioned or confronted.

Bob was not always a by-the-book type of policeman. When a young person got into minor trouble, he would sometimes allow them leniency but not before they had been given a good scare. After talking with the parents he would lock the youth in one of the empty city jail cells and leave them for several minutes. Upon his return he would ask, "How does it feel to be locked up without hope of escape? Well, if you don't stop acting like you did tonight, you are going to get a whole lot more of that feeling. Now get out of here, and I don't want to see your ugly face around here again. Ever!" It was agreed that the parents would not mention that they had been contacted. Bob knew this was a very effective lesson for most kids since he had received the same treatment when he was young. As the years passed, he was very grateful that someone cared enough to teach him what could result from his irresponsible actions. During his career in law enforcement he had seen the effect that five or ten minutes of unthinking acts could have on people's lives. If he could redirect someone's path in the right direction, he felt justified in relaxing the rules of law enforcement.

Bob's work day generally started with a trip by his office at City Hall to see if anything unusual had occurred during the night. Afterwards, he would drop in at Don's Café to have his morning cup of coffee. Also, he could measure the pulse of the city and catch up on the latest news being discussed by the customers.

Bob finished his coffee and returned to the office. There had been a report of domestic violence, and one of the deputies had responded. Bob's first thought was of Carol and Gil Walters. It would not be the first time they had been called to their house to calm Gil down when he had overindulged. Bob was very fond of Carol, and they had been friends since she was a little girl. He was relieved to hear that the report had not come from her address. He felt sorry for Carol, since she was married to what he privately referred to as a "scum sucking dog." No one knew exactly what that meant, but they were sure it was not meant as a compliment.

Carol's marriage to Gil Walters had not been pleasant. At first they were happy, but after several months of married life, Gil's attitude began to change. He began to drink excessively and was particularly mean when he was drunk. Carol was young and a very attractive woman with an extremely fine figure. If Gil saw a stranger eyeing his wife, there was always trouble. In truth, most men in town enjoyed looking at her as long as their girlfriends, wives, or Gil were not around. Carol had never encouraged anyone for their attention. Actually, she dressed in such a way as to hide her looks, but some things you just cannot cover entirely. The local men knew it was not in their best interest or Carol's to be too friendly with her. Aside from Bob and Gil's brother Bill Walters, all of her close friends were women. Several times she had been seen with bruises on her arms. She would tell anyone who asked that she had run into a door or a cabinet. Most people pretended not to notice for fear of embarrassing her. Some very close friends had spoken to her about Gil's actions. Each time Carol would defend him saying, "Gil's abuse has not been extreme, and I'm certain that things will get better in time."

Gil was the younger brother of Bill Walters. They were as different as night and day. Bill was a fine, upstanding member of the community, and Gil was the town thug. He owned three beer joints near the Red River, just south of town. It was rumored that he sold more than hamburgers and beer, but he had never been charged with any illegal activity. His taverns were located outside the city limits and beyond Bob's jurisdiction. That was a matter for the sheriff. When Gil was involved in a business deal that required muscle, some of his employees would be called on to assist. They were known around town as Gil's Gang or "G-G" men. For the past three years Gil and his gang had been involved in every shady activity within fifty miles. He had bullied and terrorized several people in the area, but Gil was smart when he selected his victims. He would pick those who would not fight back because they were afraid or those that did not care to have the sheriff investigating their activities.

Bob's relationship with Gil was somewhat civil, mainly because he did not want to cause problems for Carol. Gil did not think much of the chief but was polite toward him for obvious reasons. Bob longed for the day when he could lock Gil up and throw the key away, but when the opportunity came, the victim would either not press charges or not be willing to testify. Gil's violent actions and reputation was becoming more serious and widespread. Bob knew that one day he would go too far.

After completing his day's work, Bob instructed deputy Hank Green, and the three-night shift personnel to "Keep a close watch on the Saturday night activities and to call him if anything unusual happened." Otherwise, he would see them in the morning before church. Bob took a final drive around town and went home to enjoy what he knew would be a fine supper with his wife, Jane, and their two children, Joe and John. After eating, the family generally would walk several blocks around the neighborhood to get some exercise. Sometimes they would be joined by friends along the way. This evening was no exception. Bob took his football and threw passes to the kids as they walked. It made for stop-and-go walking, but everyone seemed to enjoy it. He dreamed about his two boys becoming star players for Hugo High and possibly going to the college ranks. His dream was dimmed a little when his youngest expressed a desire to play in the band. Bob was, at first, repulsed by this idea, but later decided that it would be all right if that's what John really wanted. However, he would continue to throw him passes, just in case. Daylight was just about gone when they arrived back at the house. It was time for the kids to take their baths and lay out their clothes for Sunday church. Bob wanted to repair a cabinet door before going to bed. Jane had asked him to fix it several weeks ago, and he thought his excuses were just about exhausted. With the cabinet work completed and all was ready for Sunday, Bob turned off the lights commenting, "It's been a great day."

Sundays in Hugo are usually quiet with many of the citizens attending the church of their choice. Some of the remaining people would be doing chores or sleeping late after a big evening at one of the late-night entertainments. Bob attended the Baptist Church where he worked with the youth group. Coach Parker and several members of the football team also attended regularly. This Sunday before the worship services began, the coach and players were asked to stand so they could be recognized for their fine play Friday night, winning the district title. The general topic of the sermon was overcoming problems and being victorious in life, even when things seemed hopeless. The timing of that sermon topic and Friday's football game was not lost on the congregation. Bob's mind wandered back to the day before at Don's Café when the boys were asked how they overcame the supposed superior team and what Coach Parker had told them." Almost everyone answered, "Coach Parker didn't say anything to us. We were mad! Friday at school each member of the team received a package which was delivered to us by the postman delivered right to our classes!!! The package contained a powder-puff with the score written on it Idabel 50 Hugo 0. The postmark was from Idabel so we knew who sent them. If those guys thought we were a bunch of powder-puffs, they don't think it now. We showed them!"

Bob would just smile when they told what had inspired them. He knew who had really sent the packages. Coach Parker had asked him to drive the forty-five miles to mail the packages from the Idabel post office. Someday the true story may be told, but it would not come from the Chief of Police. Coach Parker had said more to them than they thought. The sermon contained many comparisons between life and a football game. Bob noticed the youth were listening to every word without the usual passing of notes, whispering, and restlessness.

The following day Bob had just finished supper when the phone rang. Before he could say hello, his deputy spoke,

"There's a wreck on the highway east of town."

"Do you know who's involved?" Bob asked.

"No. And we're not sure it's inside the city limits. The caller who reported the accident was uncertain of her location. Anyway, I have dispatched a unit along with an ambulance. Do you want to go?"

"Yes, I'll take a run out there and see if I can help. Have you notified the sheriff's office?" Bob asked.

"No. Not yet, but I'm going to do that now. I wanted you to know before I call him," the deputy replied.

"These things seem to happen every year when we have our first snow." Bob mumbled under his breath. "I don't know when the people around here are going to learn how to drive on snow." Approaching the location of the wreck, Bob was aware that he was outside the city limits. He would not have an official part in the investigation. He drove several yards beyond the place where a car had gone off the side of the highway. Bob knew other emergency vehicles would need room to maneuver. He would assist the ambulance crew or perform traffic control until the sheriff and his people arrived.

When Bob got out of his patrol car, he left the emergency light on to signal danger to any oncoming traffic. As he walked toward the location of the wreck, his flashlight highlighted some car tracks in the snow along the side of the road. The tracks indicated that two cars had been parked. The front car tracks appeared to have been blocking the other car. It had been parked at an angle that would have prevented the other car from moving forward. There were several foot prints in the immediate area. Bob didn't take time to look closely at the prints but did notice that the smaller prints had a triangle-shaped logo on the heel.

69

Although what he had just seen was interesting, his thoughts quickly turned to the problem of the wreck.

He stopped at the spot where the vehicle had left the road. There was a deep drop off from the highway, and the car had traveled several feet downward before striking a large tree. The deputy and medical attendants had worked their way down to the wreck. Bob could see light coming from inside the car. He yelled down to find out if the driver was hurt and if there were other passengers in the car.

"Driver appears to be dead and there are no passengers. We're getting ready to come up. When I holler, take hold of the rope we left up there and pull," came the reply.

While Bob was waiting, he looked at the tracks the car made as it went over the embankment. There was no sign of skidding. There were foot prints with the same triangle logo on the heel that he had seen several yards up the road. A closer look revealed that the left foot print had a small grooved cut near the big toe area of the sole. A shout "Pull us up!!" came from below. Bob put his flashlight away, grabbed the rope, and began to pull. Two men from the Sheriff's Department arrived and joined in. By the time the rescue party had reached the road, the sheriff had arrived. Others arriving included a reporter from the local newspaper and several teenagers who were looking for some excitement. A group gathered around the stretcher while the medical personnel did another exam before loading the body in the ambulance.

The reporter asked, "Do you know who it is?"

"Gil Walters," they answered.

A hush fell over the crowd. The sheriff dispersed the crowd and called for a wrecker to recover the car. He spoke to Bob about notifying Gil's wife. "I can go see Carol, but you're such good friends, it may be better if you told her. What do you think, Bob?"

"I think you're right. If you don't mind, I'll go by and pick up my wife. Carol may need someone to stay with her tonight."

The sheriff agreed, "That's a good idea, and I'll go by the hospital. We don't want to tell her anything until a doctor has had a look at him. I want to be sure Gil is officially pronounced dead before we do anything. I'll give you a call on the radio."

CHAPTER 15

* * *

Notification Visit

Bob did not know what to expect inside as they rang the doorbell. Word travels fast in a small town, and someone may have already phoned with the news of Gil's death. Carol invited them into a dimly-lit living room. She was dressed in a house robe. Her head was wrapped in a towel which hung over one side of her face. It was obvious she had just gotten out of the shower. There was no indication that she was aware of the accident. She said how nice it was for them to drop by and offered them a cup of tea.

"We're ok, thank you, Carol. I'm afraid I have bad news."

"What do you mean, Bob?"

"Gil was killed tonight in a car wreck east of town. His car went off the road and struck a tree. Bob paused then continued, "They've taken his body to the hospital and are awaiting your instructions as to what you want to do."

Carol said nothing but broke down and began to cry. As Bob's wife consoled her, the towel which had been around Carol's head fell to the floor.

Jane exclaimed, "What has happened to you? Who did this? Did

Gil do this to you?" she asked. One side of Carol's face was bruised and badly swollen.

"Yes, he hit me with his fist and kicked me. My side hurts, and I think I may have a broken rib." Bob could not hide his anger. He had felt bad earlier that evening when he remembered how he hated Gil and things he had said about him. He had determined not to think or speak ill of the dead, but after seeing Carol's face, his resolution went out the window. The guilty feeling he had experienced when Gil's death was announced had vanished.

"Get her coat. We're taking her to the hospital."

On the way to the hospital Carol told them that Gil had been drinking and had accused her of an affair. "I thought he was going to kill me."

Bob said without thinking, "If I get my hands on that guy, I'm going to give him a beating he won't forget."

While Carol was being examined, the sheriff told Bob that he was having an autopsy ordered on Gil's body. "I'm also impounding the car for a complete going over. I think it's necessary under the circumstances—you know, because of the nature of Gil's business and all the enemies he had. I just want to be sure this was an accident."

Bob agreed, "I think you're right. I had intended to show you some foot prints around the location where his car left the road, but they were destroyed by all the activity. I saw the same tracks up the road. Perhaps we can go out there later tonight or tomorrow and see if they're still there."

There was plenty of conversation at Don's Café the next day. The news of an autopsy being performed on Gil's body had created much speculation among the town's people. Everyone had a theory. They ranged from accidental death to murder. Hugo had lost many important citizens in the past, but this was different. In this case there was little or no mourning. The greatest emotion seemed to be one of relief. It wasn't that the people wanted Gil dead, but as long as someone had to die, it may as well be him. This would certainly be a major topic of discussion for many months no matter what the results of the investigation revealed.

Bob didn't stop by the café the next morning. He knew what the subject of conversation would be and did not want to get involved. He dropped by later that afternoon for coffee and pie.

Don said, "We missed you this morning. Boy!! You should have been here. The case of Gil's demise was solved several times."

Bob commented, "I'm sure it was. That's why I wasn't here. I didn't want to answer a lot of questions. I told my staff to keep their thoughts on that subject to themselves. I hope they were not involved in any of that crime-solving session."

The day of Gil's funeral finally arrived. There had been some delay because of the autopsy. As the hearse made its way through down town, Carol noticed the empty streets when she passed Don's Café. There had been a heavy snow the night before, and a cold wind was blowing. Even so, she thought it strange that no one was seated at the community round table. Surely the regular coffee drinkers and town scholars would not let a little bad weather keep them from exchanging their jokes and solutions of local and world problems. Her thoughts returned to the difficult task facing her. Her husband of three years was to be buried today.

"I wonder how I will react at the church. Will I cry? What will people think if I fail to show sorrow?" She wondered if the black veil would cover the bruises she had received from Gil's last and final beating. "Oh well, no one will be there anyway. Bill and his wife, Bob and Jane will probably be the only ones there. Gil was not well liked to say the least." She recalled how long it had been since she was inside the church. She had attended regularly prior to her marriage. To the best of her recollection, it had been about two and a half years. Gil did not think much of the idea of her going to church and would get angry each time she went. When the church was in sight, it was obvious why the streets had been bare. Apparently everyone in town was there. Ushers were telling late comers, "There's standing room only."

Carol did cry that day. She cried not so much for her loss but because of the love, friendship, and understanding being expressed to her. It had been a long time since she had felt those emotions. The people did not like Gil, but they loved Carol and had not been allowed to show it. Hugo had turned out that day in support of Carol.

CHAPTER 16

✪ ✪ ✪

The Hearing

It was fortunate that district court was just about to get underway. All the personnel and necessary facilities would be available for an immediate hearing. Judge J.P. Carr would preside. "I have a full docket in the weeks ahead, and I would like to complete this preliminary hearing as soon as possible. I don't want any unnecessary delays. Remember this is a hearing so there is no need for formal, long-winded speeches." He knew, with a crowded court room, the county attorney would take the opportunity to use his vote-getting oratory. "We'll be very informal. Are you ready to present your findings?"

The attorney indicated he was ready and addressed the court to explain the purpose of the hearing and briefly outline the number of witnesses that he expected to testify.

The Judge responded, "Thank you. Call your first witness."

The sheriff was called and sworn in for questioning. "Sheriff, from your notes, and in your own words, describe the events that occurred on the evening of 11 November this year as they relate to the death of Gil Walters."

The sheriff opened his notebook and began, "I was informed by the local police at seven forty-five on the evening of 11 November that a wreck had occurred on Highway 70 east of town. A car, which was later determined to belong to Gil Walters, had run off the highway, down an embankment, and hit a tree. The paramedic at the scene did a preliminary exam and indicated that no sign of life was apparent. Later, at the hospital Doctor Roberts pronounced Gil dead. I impounded the car for investigation and called for an autopsy. The next of kin was notified that evening."

The sheriff paused and sipped from a glass of water before continuing, "I retraced Gil's movements the day of the wreck." The sheriff continued his testimony giving a detailed report of Gil's movements which included time, location, and persons coming in contact with Gil. "The last two persons known to have seen Gil alive were Gary Wallace and Howard Davis." With that statement the sheriff concluded the report of Gil's movements and began to describe the condition of the car.

"The car was checked for fingerprints. None were found that could not be explained. The front of the car was damaged as you can see in these photos. Notice the windshield is broken on the driver's side. The steering wheel is bent. The left front tire is flat, and this is attributed to the collision with the tree. There was no indication of a flat from the tire marks on the highway. The right front head light was still on. This aided the rescue party locating the wreck. The brakes appeared to be in working order. As you can see in this picture there was an open can of beer and a fifth of whiskey found in the front floorboard. The beer can was empty and the whiskey bottle was approximately half full. A few articles of clothing were found in the back seat, all of which belonged to Gil."

The sheriff fumbled with his notes then continued, "There was no sign of skidding where the car went over the embankment. There were some footprints in the snow at that location, but they were destroyed by the persons in the recovery party. It is assumed that they belong to the person who called the police department to report the wreck. We have not been able to identify the person who called. We do know it was a woman. The call was probably made from the pay phone outside the Cottonwood Club."

"That is all I have to report on the investigation except I was notified that Dr. Johnson had completed the autopsy last week. He will give the coroner's report." The county attorney dismissed the sheriff, but he was subject to recall.

"I call Gary Wallace to the witness stand."

"Mr. Wallace, did you meet with Mr. Gil Walters on the afternoon of 11 November this year?"

"Yes, I did."

"Tell the court the circumstance surrounding that meeting."

"He came by my garage around two o'clock that afternoon. He had been drinking and was obnoxious as usual. He said there was a leak in the brake lines and wanted it fixed. I told him to take it somewhere else because I didn't have time to fix it. Then he pulled that tough guy routine on me and said he would be back in two hours, and the leak better be fixed. He also made a comment about my sixteen-year-old daughter. After that comment, I wasn't about to fix his brakes. He left his car parked in front with the keys in the ignition. He came back around four or five o'clock, got in the car, and drove off. I'm sure he thought I had worked on his car. I didn't have time to tell him that I had not fixed the brakes. I'm not sure I would have even if I had had the opportunity. That was the last I saw of him."

"My next witness is Howard Davis." Before Howard could make his way to the stand, the Judge tugged at his stomach and called a fifteen-minute break.

"We will get to Mr. Davis when we resume."

After the break, Howard began his testimony. "Gil arrived at my place around six fifteen that evening. The attorney interrupted and asked Howard to identify "his place." I own the Cottonwood Club. I had not opened yet. He knocked on the front door for a few minutes, but when I didn't open up, he came through the side door. He was about three sheets in the wind." The attorney stopped Howard again and asked him to explain what he meant by "three sheets in the wind."

"It means drunk. Everybody knows that! As I was saying, he came in the side door and began to question me about Carol's visits. I told him she had been here earlier but had been gone about thirty minutes. He was mad that she had been visiting. She visits mostly with my wife. Of course, Gil tried to make something nasty out of it. As if Carol would have anything to do with an old—aaah—fellow like me. We are friends, and that's all. He told me if I didn't put a stop to it, I might find my place burned to the ground with me and mine in it. He grabbed the can of beer I had sitting on the bar and stormed out the door. I had put some sedative in that beer, but I didn't tell him. Then he left, and I was glad to see him go. That was around six thirty. I know because I was just about ready to open up."

This was new information to the attorney. "Why on earth did you put sedative in the beer, Howard?"

"Everybody knows my old tom cat. He's really not mine, but he hangs around the place. He goes out tom-cat'n around at night and gets into fights with other tom cats, I suppose. He came out on the short end of the stick and was chewed up bad. He's wild as a March hare so, I decided to put sedative in his nightly beer. I figured it's the only way I could catch him to take him to the vet. He's a good mouser, and I would hate to lose him. I was just about to pour it in the cat's bowl when Gil came in."

"Why didn't you tell Gil there was sedative in the beer?"

"Well, I would have if I could have stopped him or if he had offered to pay for it. That was stealing as far as I'm concerned. I worried about it for a minute or so, and then figured that sleep might the best thing for him in his condition. If that had anything to do with the wreck, I'm sorry."

"What kind of sedative did you put in the beer, Howard?"

Howard reached into his pocket, "It's a prescription my wife has for sleeping. I have the bottle here. You can see it." He gave the prescription bottle to the attorney and started to leave the witness stand.

"One more question before you're through, Howard. Did you see anyone in or near the pay phone outside your club the evening of 11 November?"

"No. I didn't," replied Howard.

"Thank you. That will be all. You can sit down."

The next testimony was what everyone was waiting for, the coroner's report.

"Gil Walters died from massive internal injuries and a severe blow to the head. There were cuts about the face and neck. Glass from the windshield was embedded in the head wound and face. There were bruises around the chest and shoulder area. The cause of death was severe internal injuries to the chest area. It appeared the injury was caused by contact with the steering column." Dr. Johnson presented photographs and x-rays to the court showing the injuries he was describing. He stated the alcohol content of his blood was well over the amount to be considered intoxicated. The estimated time of death was between six and seven o'clock. "The injuries are consistent with those I have seen in the past resulting from the head-on collision of two automobiles."

The county attorney continued, "Take a look at this prescription for sedatives and tell the court if you are familiar with this drug." Dr. Johnson indicated he had prescribed that drug many times and was familiar with its effects. The doctor was asked, "How quick does the drug take affect? Would the test you did on Gil's blood check for drugs of this type?"

After a moment's pause the Doctor answered, "The drug's effect would vary with each person and situation. I can't give you a time. Yes, the test I ran on Gil's blood would indicate the presence of this drug if it was there."

The attorney approached the witness and asked, "Was there any presence of this drug or any other?" That question created a stir throughout the court room.

"No, there was not." The sigh of relief coming from Howard Davis could be heard throughout the halls of the old court house.

After conferring with the sheriff, the attorney told the judge he had an additional witness. It would be the last witness to be called, but he was not in court.

"The sheriff can have him here in fifteen minutes if we have a recess."

The judge agreed to break for lunch, reconvene at one thirty, and the witness would be heard at that time. The missing witness turned out to be John Allen who worked at the A-1 Brake Service Company. The attorney started his questioning,

"Mr. Allen, it is my understanding that you checked the brakes on the wrecked automobile which belonged to Gil Walters. Is that correct?"

"Yes, I did", replied John.

"Did you check the level of the brake fluid?"

"Yes, it was low, but the brakes were still in working order. There was enough fluid to pressure up the system."

"Thank you. You can get back to work, and I appreciate you getting here on such short notice." The county attorney concluded, "Your Honor, that's all of the testimony we have to present. Do you have any further questions?"

The judge rubbed his chin, leaned back in his chair, and looked as if he were in deep thought. He told the attorney to approach the bench. "I was wondering why you didn't call Carol Walters as a witness." The attorney explained that he and the sheriff had questioned her thoroughly and felt that she could add nothing new to the investigation. He indicated they didn't want to put her through any more stress but offered to call her. "No, I don't think it's necessary. Take your seat." the judge answered.

Addressing the entire court, the judge stated, "I believe it's very clear that this was an accident. An accident with extenuating circumstances, that is, since there was alcohol involved. But, none-the-less, an accidental death, and that's my ruling. Gil Walters's death is ruled accidental. I cannot close this hearing without saying this. Howard Davis, you better be more careful about that tomcat's beer. You were lucky that Gil did not drink any of it. If that sedative had shown up in his blood, we could be seeing a lot of each other. This hearing is adjourned."

CHAPTER 17

* * *

The Shopping Trip

There was little excitement around town, and time seemed to drag. Bob called an 0800 meeting for the entire staff. "We have had it easy for about two months. This is about to change. There are several items we should discuss regarding coming events. Item number one: weather forecasts indicate we are in for an unusually cold and wet winter. As usual when there is snow or ice on the streets, we will check on our older citizens to insure they have adequate heat and food. I have a list from last year. Everyone look it over and add anyone that I may have missed. Cathy, since you are the dispatcher, you will call each person every other day when weather is bad. Remember, we don't want to get into the taxi or heating business, but we can get them help if they need it. Item two: we will be getting two new patrol cars. We will trade in the oldest with all the damaged fenders. That will give us a total of five good cars, and that should be enough."

Deputy Hank Green interrupted and said, "Bob, it may be a good time to tell the new deputies about your experience with Mrs. Land and our new patrol car sometime back."

"That is a great suggestion," Bob replied. "I'll do just that. I had just received our new patrol car. It had colorful markings unlike cars in the past. I was very proud and was driving around town showing it to anyone who would take the time to look. I was on my way to the office when I saw Mrs. Land coming from the opposite direction several blocks away. Her driving ability is well known throughout town, and everyone recognizes her red Oldsmobile immediately.

She is short of stature, and even though she had pillows in the driver's seat, her view of the road was through the steering wheel. It appeared at times that there was no driver at all. Her top speed was less than twenty-five miles per hour. To a stranger, it looked as if an empty car was rolling slowly down the street.

As our cars were approaching one another, I pulled over to the curb and came to a complete stop. I felt helpless as I watched the Oldsmobile glance off my new front left fender. After the initial shock and a brief moment of anger, I got out on the passenger side to look at the condition of the cars. There was not much damage since Mrs. Land was in the process of braking at the time of the collision. She remained seated while I did the inspection.

I reported, "It looks like you and I are going to be visiting the body shop tomorrow."

Mrs. Land kept repeating, "It was my fault. It was my fault."

I assured her it was not her fault.

"No. It was my fault, Chief Mitchell."

I replied, "No, Mrs. Land, it was my fault. I saw you coming three blocks away and had two opportunities to turn off, and I didn't. It was my fault. Now, you go home and drive real careful."

She is such a sweet elderly lady I could not stay mad. I just laughed and drove to the office; so, fellows, if you see a red Olds coming your way, turn off the first chance you get." The officers were laughing and looking at each other.

Bob continued his meeting, "Item three: The holidays are coming soon. We, along with the fire department, are required to decorate the downtown area. You know the routine. It will take a lot of time and effort, but we manage it every year. I will have a work schedule soon."

"Item four: office parties, we always have Thanksgiving and Christmas dinners. Cathy, I know it seems like I'm always picking on you, but would you, once again, take charge of planning and overseeing our Thanksgiving and Christmas dinners? You have done such a marvelous job in the past. You would have complete control over everything. The rest of the staff would help as you direct. I will take care of the entertainment and financing; would you agree to this?" Bob asked.

"I would agree. Actually, I enjoy doing that each year. You would have hurt my feelings if you hadn't asked," Cathy responded without hesitation.

"Wonderful! You're number one."

"Let Cathy know if you will be bringing a guest. Cathy, you should count on the mayor and his wife and as many as ten city councilmen and their guests. I had forgotten that we would have outside-the-department guests. I know I told you that you would have complete control over the planning and overseeing of the dinner. However, there is one thing I must insist on: do not let Charlie make the coffee! I don't want the department sued on the grounds of sleep deprivation." Everybody laughed.

Both parties were a total success. Everyone enjoyed the food and entertainment. A few of the outside guests expressed disappointment in not sampling Charlie's coffee. They had heard many stories about it. They were told to come by the office any work day and get a free cup; as of this date none have accepted the offer.

CHAPTER 18

✪ ✪ ✪

The Readjustment

Everyone was looking forward to spring. Carol was busy getting her late husband's business dealings settled. There was a life insurance claim to process and paperwork to complete the sale of Gil's three taverns. She had indicated to the realtor, "There is no way I will be directly or indirectly involved with the operation of those taverns. I'll accept any reasonable offer just short of giving them away." The realtor did a good job and had received fair offers on all three taverns from Gil's former employees. Carol was pleased that the weather had prohibited travel. She was not ready to visit and needed a little more time to adjust to her new situation. Bob and Jane and a few of her close friends had dropped by to see if she needed anything. They did not stay long, and that was fine with Carol.

Winter was just about over, and everyone was moving about town doing the things they had been unable to do for months. Gardeners were breaking ground for the upcoming season. City road workers were busy repairing damage created by the cold weather. Shops were displaying bathing suits and outdoor sportswear. Members of the Chamber of Commerce were planning the town's annual 4th of July picnic. It was as if the town had awakened from a deep sleep. Carol had even begun to venture outside. This presented a problem for deputy Hank Green because he wanted to ask Carol for a date but thought it might be too soon after Gil's death. He knew there would be others wanting to invite her out, and he wanted to be first. He decided he would ask Bob for guidance and to lead interference for him. Bob told him he would be talking to Carol often, and he would let him know when the time was right. He continued, "You better be nice to her, and you know what I mean. She is not going to be just another notch on your gun. If you hurt her, I will string you up by your toes. When you ask her out the first time I suggest you invite her to church. Next, you might ask her to dinner." Bob grinned and said," If she hasn't become tired of you by then, you could suggest a movie or something in Paris. I think that would be a good start."

This was not what Hank had in mind but agreed that he would follow his advice and assured Bob that he was serious about her. "You know how I have always felt about her. I had a few dates with her before she was married. I was not ready or prepared for a serious relationship at that time. It was only after she got married that I realized how much she meant to me."

At Jane's urging, Bob had spoken with Carol several times during the past few weeks. At first he and Jane were pleased with the progress she was making putting her life back in order. Carol had done a magnificent job handling the business side of her life. Now it was time to work on the social aspects. This would be more difficult for her, and she would need a push. Bob said, "Jane wants to go shopping in Oklahoma City, but I don't want her to go alone. She saw a dress advertised that she thinks she can't live without. Would you go with her? You might find something you like as well." Bob knew if anything would get a woman out of the house, it would be an opportunity to go shopping.

"Yes, I think I would enjoy taking a trip with Jane. When does she plan on going?"

Bob did not know what Jane had planned for the next few days, but he had to say something "As soon as you can go, she is ready anytime. I'll have her call you to set the date." Bob felt good that the plan was working. He would drive directly to his house and tell Jane. Knowing how his wife liked to travel and shop, he was sure she would go along with the arrangement.

Jane and Carol had completed a very successful day and half of shopping in the big city. They had just returned to their hotel room to check out when the phone rang. It was a call from Bob, "I want you to stay an extra night. We've had our usual late winter snowstorm, and the roads are bad. I think they'll be clear by tomorrow afternoon. I'll call tomorrow and let you know if it's ok to travel. I'm sure it's breaking your heart to have another half day to shop, but you'll just have to grin and bear it."

As expected, the roads were clear, and the pair returned home safely the following afternoon. Jane was anxious to model her new dress for Bob, "I know I spent more for this than I should have, but isn't it just right for church and special occasions? Remember, it was your idea for me to go shopping."

Bob smiled, "I remember. That's ok. You look beautiful."

Jane was pleased with Bob's comment and continued, "Carol bought several outfits. Just wait till you see her! She's a new woman!"

Bob was seated at his office desk when he saw Carol go by the window. She was on her way to pay her bill at the water department. He waited for her to return and went outside to invite her in for a cup of their famous coffee. He was disappointed that she was not dressed in one of her new outfits. "I thought that you would be showing off your new clothes." Carol informed Bob that men didn't know anything about women's apparel.

"The things I bought were for summer and early fall. Besides, I'm not going to take a chance on ruining my new wardrobe in this messy weather. Carol refused the coffee saying that she had heard about their coffee and didn't care to be sleepless for a week.

On the way to Carol's car, Bob informed her, "That's why I have my coffee at Don's." Carol had parked in an area that had a thin layer of snow remaining on the sidewalk. They made their parting comments, and Carol drove away. Turning to go back to his office Bob looked down at the sidewalk, and there it was. A footprint with a triangular shaped logo on the heel that was clear as day and a grooved cut near the big toe area of the left foot.

Thoughts were racing through Bob's mind, "I saw those same footprints in the snow the night Gil died. No mistake about it, she was there. Should I confront her? No, I think justice was served. I'll leave it that way. I prefer a system of justice to a legal system any day. Everyone in town feels the same. Still, I sure would like to know what really happened out there that night. Maybe someday I'll ask."

CHAPTER 19

✪ ✪ ✪

Something in The Air

When Bob left his house this morning, he had no idea that the day's events would include the most talked about unsolved mystery of his law enforcement career. As usual he went by his office to get the overnight activities report, "You guys are doing a good job monitoring the town's activities from this office. Now, I'll go see what's really happening in town," Bob said as he laughed and walked out the door. This was interpreted by his office staff as, "I'm going to get coffee at Don's Cafe."

A few minutes later deputy Hank Green stopped by the café to tell Bob that the high school principal had called and requested police immediately.

Hank said. "I don't know what the problem is, but the principal sure was upset."

Bob transferred his freshly-poured coffee into a paper cup and told Hank he had better follow him to school. When Bob entered the school house, he was immediately made aware of the problem. The odor of a skunk was overwhelming.

"Gee whiz! How am I going to locate and trap a skunk?" Bob thought. He had attended Hugo High, and he was aware of all the little nooks and crannies available for an animal to hide.

"I want the person or persons responsible for this to be tracked down and punished. You need to question these three students. I have no idea if they are guilty, but based on the past, it's a good place to start your investigation," the principal stated while handing Bob the list of names. Bob was taken to the location where the skunk was found. He was relieved to find that the skunk had already been removed from the building.

Bob interviewed several students but made little progress. He reported his findings to the principal, "I haven't seen so many wide-eyed, innocent faces. I think the best thing to do is wait a few days and question some of them again. You know whoever did this won't be able to keep quiet."

Bob was amused by the incident and murmured to himself as he returned to the café "Why didn't I think of doing that when I was in school?"

The leads were few and the investigation was placed on hold. Bob knew it might be years before the secret would be revealed.

Bob had just returned to his office and was relating his experience at the high school when he received a phone call from Tony Gilbert, the town veterinarian, "Someone broke into my office last night and stole several items. I'm not sure what they got yet; I'm still looking. Can you come over right away?" Tony asked excitedly.

Bob said, "Don't let anyone into your office until I get there. We want to keep the crime scene intact. I am on my way; I'll be there in just a few minutes."

As Bob and Deputy Green were driving over there, Bob thought to himself, "My word; what is going on? There must have been a full moon last night. Already two different events have occurred, and it's not even ten o'clock. I wonder what the rest of the day will be like." By the time they arrived at his office, Tony and his wife had a pretty good list of the stolen items.

"Doctor, can you tell me the approximate value of the property taken? "

"I have several belt buckles that I won in rodeo events that probably amount to a few thousand dollars. But the main thing I am concerned with were some of the medical items that were taken. They could be very dangerous if used by a human being. It would affect sexual functions and could be very dangerous," stated Tony.

"You can fill me in on that later. Right now I'm concerned with catching who did this. He must have come in through the window because he stepped in some cow manure and tracked it across the floor. How many calves do you have in that little pen next to your office?" Bob inquired.

"I only have one out there. It has a communicable disease, and I'm treating it with some new medicines to see what effect it will have, but I only have one right now."

"But, yes, you are right, it would appear that he got his boots in the wrong spot," Tony stated.

Bob and his deputy checked for finger prints around the window and other areas that were obviously involved. They found smudges, but nothing of any value. He told the deputy to take pictures and measure the footprints. They told the doc that they would continue to work on the case and be in contact with him on any progress they made. Later that morning Bob left his office and went to the café to have coffee. Several of the usual crowd were present. He noticed one guy in particular who was always hanging out there. He was sort of a drug-store cowboy, and he dressed like all the cowboys and talked the same talk, but he was never known to be around any cattle or horses. Apparently, he liked that lifestyle and wanted everyone to think he was a cowboy.

Bob noticed what appeared to be a very small amount of dried manure on his left boot, and that was very unusual because he was always clean and neat; even his blue jeans were pressed. No one really knew what he did for a living, and any dirt on his boots was certainly suspicious; however, it got Bob to thinking about a plan, and he needed help from his friends and several people to put his plan into effect. He returned to the veterinarian office and asked two of his friends to meet him there. When everyone had arrived at the doc's office, he had them sit down. "I think I might know who did this; however, I'm not certain by any means. I have a plan here I would like to put into place just to see if my suspicion is correct. And I'm going to need your help."

"Doc, that medicine you're giving that calf, would that show up in the manure if we had it checked?" Bob inquired of the doctor.

"Yes, I believe it would. We would have to send it to Oklahoma City to get complete results. But I think it would show up," stated Dr. Tony.

"Well, here is what I want to do. I want you guys to be scattered around town; one of you should be in the barber shop next door and the other should be in the café. I don't know which area my suspect will be in," stated Bob. "I'm going to come by and take a swab from each of your left boots. If the suspect is in the area, I want you to ask me what I'm doing. I also want you to say that you have just cleaned your boots," Bob instructed. "I will say it doesn't matter when your boots were cleaned. The test I'm performing will show up either way," stated Bob. "I'm going to send the swabs to OSBI in Oklahoma City. It will take one day to get them up there and one day to get them back. Bob paused, "Hopefully, we can solve this mystery in two days. If my plan works the way I intend, the suspect will leave immediately to dispose of evidence or try to hide his left boot, and we will have surveillance on the suspect's property," said Bob. "Well, everyone, that's my plan. What do you think about it?" Bob questioned.

Some laughed and said, "We didn't think you were that smart."

Bob left and went by the grocery store and bought Q tips and several small fruit jars. When everyone arrived in their proper places, Bob entered the café. He approached his friend and told him he would need a sample from his left boot. His friend loudly asked what he had been instructed to say. Bob took several samples and placed them in separate jars with the boot owner's name. He proceeded to do the same thing for everyone in the café. As expected, Bob's suspect, McAdams, along with others, left immediately. Bob was pleased that several left at the same time because he had not indicated to his friends or the doctor who he thought had committed the crime. He did not want to accuse the wrong person.

Bob slowly followed McAdams to his home, hoping his theory was wrong since McAdams was well-liked by everyone who knew him, including himself. The deputies were already in place to observe McAdams' actions once he arrived. McAdams hurriedly entered his house and returned immediately to his truck carrying several boxes. He got back into his pickup truck and quickly exited the property. The deputy followed a short distance before he performed a traffic stop for a broken tail light. As the deputy approached the driver, he noticed the stolen items in the back of the truck. Several of the doctor's medicine vials were labelled, and he knew immediately it was part of the stolen property at which time the deputy made an arrest. All of the stolen property was recovered, and charges were filed against McAdams.

Dr. Tony was relieved and pleased that everything was recovered, especially the medicine he was so concerned about. He told Bob that news of solving this crime would be a great help in furthering Bob's career.

Dr. Tony indicated he thought Bob should run for sheriff. The doc said, "I deal with people outside the city limits all the time; everyone in the county is going to know how quickly and professionally you solved this crime."

Bob stated he wished the details of his plan would not be revealed until after the trial. Tony agreed. Later investigations of McAdams' home revealed several items that had been stolen from towns as far as 65 miles away. He was later found guilty of robbery and sentenced to five years in the state penitentiary.

CHAPTER 20

✪ ✪ ✪

The Election

An event occurred every four years that divided the citizens into several groups. The division began when it was time to elect a new mayor. The same three men always filed for the office: Mr. Smith, Mr. Little, and Mr. Howard. They were successful businessmen, and each had won the office at least once. Nowhere was the division more apparent than morning coffee at Don's Café. Friends who normally had their coffee together now occupied separate tables discussing strategies for their candidate's campaign. This year an additional candidate had entered the race. Others had entered the race before, so it was not surprising that there would be four running for the office. The shock was who had filed: Benny Wills! He was considered by many to be the town clown. He was well known for his unusual and somewhat wacky ideas. His wife Betty was a nice person. However, she was withdrawn and didn't have many friends. At times she seemed to be embarrassed by her husband's antics. Most of the town's people felt sorry for her.

The candidates had debates, tea parties, rallies, and public speeches around town. Signs were displayed in front yards and on telephone poles. You would have thought they were running for President of the United States. But there were other races also which created excitement and drew people's attention—that being the race for sheriff and county commissioner. As a rule all the races were hotly contested but were done in a respectful and dignified manner.

There was an incident that occurred in the race for county commissioner that required immediate attention. A public meeting was called to discuss and resolve the problem: Bob Mitchell had taken control of the podium and was acting as Master of Ceremonies. He called the meeting, and no one knew exactly why. Most of the people may have thought it was a political campaign, but it wasn't. "I want to call your attention to both of the men I have on each side of me. Off to my right I have Jerry Nelson, which you all know, and to my left is Brian Seymour. They are both running for the office of County Commissioner," stated Bob.

Bob continued, "Both of these men are well qualified. I know their qualifications because I have seen them in action. I've seen them from Iwo Jima to Guadalcanal to who-knows-where, all the islands all the way to Japan. They are well equipped with the knowledge of how to build the roads that are much needed around here. The only difference is that here, they hopefully won't be shot at while they work. At any rate, I just wanted to reiterate they are both well qualified, highly respectable people with great character, and they are both running for the same office. You know as guys come back from the war, jobs are not all that plentiful, and both of these men need a job. Now there is a situation that has come up here that needs to be handled," Bob stated. "I know that most of you have seen the printed flyers that have been distributed around town. I will not describe it because I know most of you have seen it. It has some derogatory remarks and comparisons. We know Seymore's sister has some problems. This was the dirtiest political trick I have ever seen. This is a small town; we don't need this kind of campaigning going on in our town. This is what today's meeting is about. Both of these men talked this over. They both agreed to this meeting. In fact, they both asked me to call this meeting. They both have something to say. I wish to give them the opportunity to speak their peace. I don't want any interruptions from anybody out there. After they have both spoken, if anyone has any questions, that's fine, we will get to them, but while they are talking, please be quiet. OK, now who wants the microphone first?"

Jerry takes the microphone first and states, "Thank you, Bob, for calling this meeting and for giving Brian and myself the opportunity to discuss this filthy advertisement. First, I wanted to say, I did not submit that advertisement, and I want that perfectly clear. Second, if I thought for one minute that I won an election due to an advertisement like that, I would resign immediately! I think it is terrible when two men who have been friends most of their lives are depicted in an ad as mortal enemies. Each of us has a campaign strategy and have been running it decently and never saying a bad word about the character or quality of the other person. We were in different outfits in the military, but we built roads and tore down roads, built bridges and tore down bridges; we worked from one end of the Japanese islands to the other. We were also in the European campaign to some extent; however, it was winding down by the time we joined the military. Most of our experience was in the Far East, but I do know Brian is a qualified man who would make us a good County Commissioner. If I did say something about him, I would have nothing but praise and admiration. That's the way I feel. Each of us will speak about our own qualifications and let you be the judge. Something like this coming up is beyond my wildest nightmares. It saddens my heart and will always put a damper on this election. I want to hear nothing but the positive things each of us can bring to the office. Now, Brian, is it OK if I tell this now? (Brian begins nodding his head). We agreed ahead of time that it would be. I must tell you that regardless of how this election turns out, whichever man gets elected plans to hire the other in his organization. So, we both plan to go to work for everyone here. Don't feel bad voting for one or the other as we both will end up with a job from this election. Now Brian, are you ready to take the mic?"

"Yes, I am", stated Brian as he approached the podium. "I appreciate your kind words, Jerry. My name is Brian Seymour. Most of you have known me most of my life. I am saddened and shocked at what has transpired here. I think most of you know that my sister is mentally retarded. She is a sweet girl; she does her best, but some things she just doesn't understand. I will say she is not here to be made fun of. I will fight any man that I know of that is doing that! I too have attempted to find out the origination of the fliers, but have been unsuccessful. I don't think they were printed in Hugo. I think all three of us attempted to obtain this information, to no avail. Someday we will find out the truth."

Bob chimed in at this point, "I know I asked for no interruptions, but I can't contain myself. I want you boys to know that if we do find out, we'll flip a coin to see who takes that person behind the barn, and whoever takes him back there is not going to come back with much. I can tell you that for sure!"

"Thank-you, Bob," stated Brian. "I appreciate everyone helping me to protect my darling sister. I love her to death and frankly, I wouldn't have her any other way. She is as sweet as she can be, and she does her best, which is good enough for me. There are people who make fun of her. Those are very small people in my book, and one of these days, it will come back on them. You know my mother always said, there but for the grace of God go I, and she could just as well be your sister or mother. God has a purpose for her, and He will lead her to find it. Now I want to express my appreciation for my opponent and state his qualifications are every bit as good as mine. I have nothing but admiration for his character and feel assured he would be able to do a good job. I guess that is all we came to say at this meeting. That is all I have to say, so I'm turning the microphone back over to Bob. Bob, I appreciate you calling this meeting and bringing this all to light."

Bob took the microphone and said, "We don't know how many were printed, but we have recovered 23. If you find one, please destroy it or turn it in to one of us. I really don't want Brian's sister to see them. She may not understand them now, but some day she might, and I just prefer she never sees them. I'm sure you don't wish for her to see them either. I know most of the people in this town and in this county have a good heart, and they don't want to hurt anybody. Now, has anyone got anything they would like to say?"

One person got up and stated, "I had my mind made up about which one of these men I was going to vote for, and now I have no idea! What I would like to do is elect both of them!"

Bob said, "Well, unfortunately, there is only one job available, but I am glad you feel that way about both of them. And I guarantee you, either way you will have a great county commissioner. I guess if you already had your mind made up which way you wanted to vote, don't let this stupid, idiotic advertisement change your mind!" Bob continued, "I said this wasn't going to be a political rally, but I am running for Sheriff, and so far, my opponent and I have managed to keep a clean mud-slinging-free campaign going, and I am sure we will continue to do that. I see around town that some of the campaigns are getting a little bit negative, and I hope after this will they see what can happen with mud-slinging, and then all the dirty tactics will stop. We don't need this in a small town. Everybody knows everybody; everyone knows their character; everyone knows what they have done and what they haven't done. None of us are perfect, but mud-slinging, particularly in a small town, rarely does any good. I would appreciate it if not only those affected here, but every other campaign in this area is run in a clean fashion like this country has never seen before. I appreciate ya'll being here today. If you have any questions down the line, give us a holler, and we'll try to answer them. Thank-you and good night. One other thing I would like to say is that the three of us may have used a word or two that we shouldn't have about this incident. We have been so upset. We may have used incorrect language. Please forgive us if we did do this. Anyway, forgive us if we did, congratulate us if we didn't. Thank-you.

Several days after the meeting, the election was held, and Seymour was elected county commissioner. As promised, Jerry was hired as his main assistant. The two men alternated running and getting elected for that office for seven four-year terms. It was certainly a good time for Hugo and the county because Hugo had the best roads anywhere in the state. The extra newspapers were never found, and his sister was given jobs around town and treated with the upmost respect. She excelled under the watchful eye of several of the townsfolk, and each job that she accepted had a little more responsibility, and she handled them all well. It was a real pleasure watching her blossom into a fine young lady. She was well respected, well treated, and all was as it should have been.

One other thing occurred a week after that meeting: Bob Mitchell was elected Sheriff of the County. His friend, Bill Green, who would have been a shoo-in for Chief of Police decided to go with Bob to the County Sheriff's Department. They both had long and successful careers.

With the vote-getting work done in the mayor's race, it was time to go to the polls. Votes were counted manually and would require several hours to complete. The results would be announced the following day by John Harris, who was the chairman of the election committee.

The counting was well under way when John was informed that someone was at the door and wanted to see him. It was Benny Will's wife.

"John, I'm sorry to bother you, but I have a big problem." John could see Betty was very upset and inquired what the nature of her problem was. "I have talked to several of my friends and have not found one who voted for my husband. I love my husband, but I'm not sure he is the best person to be mayor. I must confess, I got busy and didn't vote. Anyway, I'm afraid he will only get one vote, and everyone will know even his wife didn't vote for him. He has so much fun poked at him already; he could never live that down. It didn't occur to me that he wouldn't get some votes. Will you let me vote now?"

"There's nothing I can do, Betty. Let's hope that he did better than you think," John replied in a sympathetic tone. He returned to the vote-counting but couldn't forget the agony Betty was going through.

The next morning John was ready to announce the voting results. "May I have your attention?" John shouted. "The results of the voting for mayor are as follows: Smith-1639, Little-904, Howard- 482, Wills-2." After the crowd settled, John announced, "Your new mayor is Mr. Bill Smith."

Bill came to the stage and shook hands with John and whispered, "I understood that I received 1640 votes. What happened to that other vote?"

"I took one vote from you and gave it to Benny," John answered.

"I don't know about that! What if that had changed the outcome? To take a vote that was rightfully mine and give it to someone else is not right!" Suddenly he appeared to be very angry.

"I know it's not right, but there were extenuating circumstances. I wouldn't have done it if it had affected the outcome. I can change the totals if you like," John confessed.

"What were the extenuating circumstances?" asked Smith.

"Let's put it this way- -would you rather the folks talk about your historic landslide victory for the next four years or the fact that Benny Wills wife didn't vote for him? That would sure make good conversation at Don's Café."

In deep thought, Bill rubbed his chin and replied, "You know, after all, 1639 has a nice ring to it."

CHAPTER 21

✪ ✪ ✪

Silver Dollar Trophy

With the election over and all the results tabulated, the city began to return to some normalcy. Candidates renewed their former lifestyles and actually joked about the outcomes of their races with their former competitors. It was all done in a friendly, good-natured atmosphere. Charlie Howard, a former candidate for mayor, was a practical joker. He owned a service station and grocery store along the highway at the west edge of town. It was a hangout for several members of a spit-and-whittle club whose main interest was baseball. Charlie always had his radio tuned to a baseball ball game with the volume turned up so those sitting on the benches out front could hear. This provided much entertainment. Charlie loved to sit with the men when his wife was available to look after the business inside the store. Each person had his favorite team, and they all enjoyed arguing the team of their choice.

Charlie was well known for his practical jokes. He had taken a silver dollar and welded a nail to one side. He attached the dollar to the pavement between the gasoline pumps and the front door of the store. As customers approached the store, they would see the dollar and attempt to pick it up. The dollar was firmly attached, and after a few seconds they would give up. Of course the on-lookers would not make any attempt to warn the person but got a good laugh when someone realized they had been had. It was interesting to see the different reactions from the people. Some would ask if the dollar belonged to those sitting on the benches. Others would step on the dollar and look around to see if anyone was watching. Regardless of the reaction, it was always a joke that everyone took delight in observing. Most victims were good natured and took the prank in stride.

Mayor William "Bill" Smith, Frontier Bank President, stopped to buy a loaf of bread. This was unusual since his wife did their shopping at a store downtown. Bill saw the dollar, and asked if it belonged to anyone seated on the bench. Charlie thought: "To be sitting outside at this particular time, must be a gift from heaven." His main rival for the office of mayor was about to fall for his silver dollar joke.

"No, it's not mine. Does it belong to any of you guys?" Charlie remarked. The remainder of those present indicated a lack of ownership. Bill smiled, and said, "This is my lucky day," and bent over to pick up the coin. After several attempts he gave up. The laughter was louder than usual. Charlie said, "You've got most every dollar in town, but that's one you won't get."

Bill chuckled and went inside to make his purchase.

The next day Bill was confronted with questions about the incident. Don's Cafe was buzzing with the story about the joke played on the bank president. It was obvious that everyone in town knew that their newly-elected mayor had been bested by Charlie's prank. When questioned, Bill would laugh and say, "It was a good one all right."

The following week Charlie and his buddies were sitting outside the station when a stranger pulled up in a new ford. When the driver got out, he looked like a giant. Six- foot- six- inches tall, broad shoulders, narrow hips. He spotted the dollar as he approached and asked, "Does this dollar belong to any of you?"

Charlie and the rest of the gang indicated "No".

As the man attempted to pick up the coin, there was not one peep out of the onlookers. Only a thin smile greeted the man after he gave up and started toward the door. After making a purchase inside, the stranger returned to his car and retrieved a hammer and large screw driver. It took only three or four hits with the hammer before the coin and nail could be pried from the pavement. The stranger flipped the coin in the air, smiled, put it in his pocket, and drove off.

"Why didn't you stop him, Charlie?" the guys questioned.

"You've got to be kidding! Did you see the size of that man? I wouldn't have tried if he had been empty handed. I'm dang sure not going to stop him when he's holding a hammer! Why didn't you guys stop him? I noticed you didn't laugh when he couldn't pick the darn thing up.

"We'd already told him it didn't belong to us," they reminded him.

Once again, Don's Cafe was buzzing with the story of the stranger and the coin. "Hay, Charlie, I understand you are giving away silver dollars at your station. I'm going to be out there later today and expect to get one." was a common remark. It seemed the practical joke had turned on Charlie.

A couple of weeks passed, and most had forgotten the silver dollar episode. It was agreed by everyone in town that the episode was a draw. Neither man had gained an advantage. Both Charlie and Bill had been victims and had taken the joke in a noble and gentlemanly manner. Conversation at Don's Cafe turned to other topics.

The subject was resurrected one week later when someone noticed a six-inch-square, framed, glass-encased trophy on Bill Smith's desk which contained a silver dollar with a nail welded to one side. There was an engraved notation along the base of the display which read:

Mayor's Office

Hugo, Oklahoma

"Where the streets are paved with silver"

When he was questioned about the trophy, he would reply "As a famous politician once said, 'To the victor go the spoils!' This Mayor agrees with that philosophy. He also has a nephew who is six-foot-six inches tall, drives a new Ford, and lives sixty-five miles from Hugo, close enough for an occasional visit and far enough to be a stranger."

CHAPTER 22

✪ ✪ ✪

The Truth Revealed

The Baptist Church was filled to capacity. Once again, the small town of Hugo was mourning the loss of a long-time resident. Howard Davis, the owner of the Cottonwood Club had passed away. He had been ill for just a short time, and his death was not anticipated. It seemed to most folks that it was yesterday that he was moving about town laughing and joking with everyone.

Carol was seated near the front of the church. Her mind wondered back four years to the last funeral she had attended. Her husband Gil Walters had been dead for four years. There had been many changes in her life since, but somehow, in these surroundings, it didn't seem that long ago. Seated next to her were Hank, Bob and Jane. These three people helped her get through the tough times when she needed it the most. Now they would offer assistance to Howard's wife in her time of need.

Carol invited Hank, Bob and Jane to come by her house the following day for a late breakfast. She insisted that all be present and to plan for an important discussion after they had eaten. They arrived on time. Carol had been so secretive about the purpose of the meeting, they were anxious to hear what she had on her mind.

After eating, Carol said, "Let's move into the living room where we can be more comfortable."

"If we don't get to the bottom of this soon, I'm going to bust. You fought off every attempt for discussion during our meal. I'm ready to talk," Hank stated.

"Well, I want you to listen rather than talk, but you can comment after I've told you what I have to say," Carol responded.

They were seated, and Carol began, "I have a confession to make. I could not make it until now, and you will see why in a minute. I was out there the night Gil ran off the road and was killed. I had been shopping with Howard's wife. When I dropped her off at the Cottonwood Club, I saw Gil's car and knew he was inside. I wanted to get away as fast as possible, but he saw me leaving and caught up with me. He forced me off the road and dragged me out of the car. Then he proceeded to beat me."

"You don't have to do this. It's over and done with," Bob stated.

"Yes, I do and don't interrupt me until I'm through. It's not over yet. Gil had hit me and knocked me down. I had never seen him so crazy. Of course he was drunk but never like this. He kicked me. I was just about unconscious when Howard arrived. He grabbed Gil and turned him round and told him to stop. Gil said he would get Howard next and started for him. Howard had the club he kept behind the bar and hit Gil. It seemed to daze him and brought him to his senses. Gil leaned against the car for a few minutes while Howard helped me up. He appeared to be all right, and we took him to his car to sit and rest for awhile. The minute he got in the car, he started it and took off. I followed and saw the car go off the road. I went back to get Howard. He told his wife to call the police while Howard and I went to the location where the car left the road. It was dark, and we couldn't see how to get down to it."

Carol began to cry but continued, "Howard said for me to go on home that help would be there soon. We agreed that we wouldn't mention the beating incident. At that time we didn't know Gil's condition. Afterward, when we found that he had been killed, we thought it would be best not to say anything, I mean about the fight. I couldn't say anything until now. I think Howard saved my life that night. He's gone now, and I can get this off my mind. I have always believed that the car wreck was what killed Gil, otherwise I couldn't have stood the silence."

Bob asked, "Are you through, because I have something to say?"

"No. Both you and Hank are lawmen, and I know you have a duty to enforce the law. I leave it up to you any action you feel is necessary. Now I'm through."

Bob was the first to speak. "I've known you were there all these years. I saw footprints in the snow that night and confirmed that they were yours the day after you and Jane got back from that shopping trip to Oklahoma City. You made the same prints on the sidewalk. I've wanted to ask you about it many times but felt the matter was closed. That case was not in my jurisdiction at that time, but I'm sheriff now and can speak officially. Even if you had told the whole story, no charges would have been filed. Everyone knew how Gil was, and no one would have doubted you or Howard. The worst case would have been self-defense. However, I too, feel the wreck was what killed him. I think the judge's ruling of accidental death was correct. Hank, how do you feel about it?"

"I feel the same way you do. I'm sorry she had that on her shoulders all this time. She's a brave girl."

Carol said, "Jane, do you have anything to say? What you feel means a great deal to me."

"I think you are wonderful for being a good, faithful friend to Howard all these years."

"I'm glad that all of you feel this way. It has been such a burden. Bob, because you were Chief of Police, at the time, I started for your office to confess but backed out. I guess I didn't trust you to keep silent. Turns out you were keeping my secret all along. I should have had more faith in you," as she went to Bob and gave him a big hug. Let's talk about something else." Hank said with a grin. For instance; do you have any more of those home-made cinnamon rolls? I think one more with a cup of coffee would get me by till lunch."

"Hank, you better watch out. You're going to ruin that thirty four-inch waist. If she only has one roll left, I had better have it to protect you from yourself," Bob chimed in.

"We have enough for everybody to indulge. Who would like one with their coffee?" Carol inquired as she headed to the kitchen. "I'll just have coffee," Jane answered.

Carol returned with the rolls and coffee. They sat for an hour talking about old times and changes occurring around town. It was nice for Carol to laugh and enjoy conversation again without feeling guilty.

Bob said he and Jane would have to leave, but they wanted to get together again real soon.

"This has been wonderful, like old times. Carol, we're going to have to take another trip," Jane said as she got up to leave.

"Bob, can you and Jane stay for just one minute more? I have something to say to Hank, and I want you to hear it too. Now Hank, you have been asking me to marry you for over a year, and I've said 'no, not now.' I couldn't marry you with this over my head. If you still want me after hearing my confession, my answer is 'yes.' I'll understand if you say no."

"You've got to be kidding! That's all I've dreamed of for three years. Let's go get the license now and make the announcements. I'm sure you have some plans for the wedding. We can work them out on the way!" Hank answered.

Everybody cheered.

"Hank, who's your best man? I'm available."

Bob added, "This has been one great meeting. We got good food and solved a mystery, and right now I'm getting ready to go to a wedding! Now if I can just figure out who threw the skunk in the school house, my life would be perfect."

he United States
ters